·C·R·E·O·L·E·
·H·O·L·I·D·A·Y·

**Center Point
Large Print**

**This Large Print Book carries the
Seal of Approval of N.A.V.H.**

ॐ श्री गणेशाय नमः

PHYLLIS A. WHITNEY

·C·R·E·O·L·E·
·H·O·L·I·D·A·Y·

CENTER POINT PUBLISHING
THORNDIKE, MAINE • USA

BOLINDA PUBLISHING
MELBOURNE • AUSTRALIA

This Center Point Large Print edition is published in the year
2003 by arrangement with McIntosh & Otis, Inc.

This Bolinda Large Print edition is published in the year
2003 by arrangement with McIntosh & Otis, Inc.

The text of this Large Print edition is unabridged. In other aspects, this book
may vary from the original edition. Printed in Thailand. Set in 16-point
Times New Roman type by Bill Coskrey and Gary Socquet.

US ISBN 1-58547-253-0
BC ISBN 1-74030-830-1

U.S. Library of Congress Cataloging-in-Publication Data.

Whitney, Phyllis A., 1903-
    Creole holiday / Phyllis A. Whitney.--Center Point large print ed.
    p. cm.
    Summary: In the 1890's, eighteen-year-old Lauré, after years of living with her strict aunt in New York
City, accompanies her famous actor father to New Orleans during Mardi Gras to acquaint herself with the
city where her father grew up and where she was born.
    ISBN 1-58547-253-0 (lib. bdg. : alk. paper)
    1. Large print books. 2. Large print books. [1. Family problems--Fiction. 2. Fathers and daughters--
Fiction. 3. Mardi Gras--Fiction. 4. Actors and actresses--Fiction. 5. New Orleans (La.)--History--19th
century--Fiction.] I. Title.

PZ7.W616 Cr 2003
[Fic]--dc21

                                                                                                2002067631
                              Australian Cataloguing-in-Publication.

Whitney, Phyllis A., 1903-
Creole holiday / Phyllis A. Whitney.
ISBN 1740308301
1. Large type books.
2. Actors and actresses--Fiction.
3. New Orleans (La.)--History--19th century--Fiction.
4. Family--Fiction.
5. Love stories.
I. Title.
813.6

              British Cataloguing-in-Publication is available from the British Library.

Contents

1. Harlequin Mask and Juliet Cap

THE day was cold; it was early in February and snow lay thick upon the streets of New York. At the front windows of a brownstone house in the East Thirties, a girl pressed her face to the frosty pane, yearning for spring and warmth and adventure.

Winter had been so long and so dull that Lauré Beaudine could hardly bear it. But now that her father was back in town . . . She laughed softly because she knew something that not even Aunt Judith knew.

Rubbing a clear place on the pane, she watched intently as her aunt, Miss Judith Allen, went primly down the steps and away from the house, her black mantle pulled close about her. A bonnet that was old-fashioned in these mid-nineties shielded her ears from the cold. Good! Lauré thought, watching her disappear down the street. Aunt Judith was off to visit a sick friend and she would be gone for an hour or more. It would be possible to have the house to herself for a little while.

It was cold in here, since Aunt Judith felt it a waste to light a fire in the parlor when there was no company. But Lauré did not mind as she whirled from the front windows and sped across the dimly lighted room. Eagerly she began to fling back the heavy draperies that shrouded the side windows, so that gray daylight could seep into the room. Aunt Judith never let in any more light than she could help, for fear it would fade the rugs or the red-velvet upholstery of which she was so proud. Lately Lauré had begun to hate red velvet.

Now, free of her aunt's restraining presence, Lauré pulled the bone pins from her soft blond hair and let it tumble in waves about her shoulders. Her eyes, big and dark brown, danced with the light of freedom. At eighteen she knew she was not a pretty girl—as Aunt Judith frequently reminded her. Not at all pretty in the sense that her mother, Aunt Judith's younger sister, had been pretty. This was a handicap, because an actress must give the effect of beauty before the footlights. And someday Lauré Beaudine would be a great actress. How could she fail when her father was one of the most famous Shakespearian actors in the country? Not that he had ever recognized his daughter's yearning for the stage. At least not so far. But there would come a time—and it couldn't be far away.

Having lighted the parlor to some extent, Lauré flew to the mantel and propped upon it the leather-bound volume of Shakespeare's plays she had smuggled downstairs from its hiding place in her room. Then she looked into the mirror above the cold hearth. The tilted glass gave back the reflection of a tall, slim girl with a mass of pale-gold hair framing the oval of her face, rippling over her shoulders. She stepped well back across the room so that she could watch her full-length image in the glass.

Her dress was all wrong, of course. She should be wearing a flowing gown that would serve as Lady Macbeth's night robe. But she couldn't take time for a costume now. Keeping an eye on the mirror, she moved slowly across the room with the pace of a sleepwalker, holding her hands before her, as if she washed them over and over to remove the telltale stain of blood.

" 'Yet here's a spot,' " she cried, and listened in her mind for the speech of the Doctor that would follow in the play:

" 'Hark! she speaks: I will set down what comes from her, to satisfy my remembrance the more strongly.' "

Then again she spoke the words of Lady Macbeth: " 'Out, damned spot! out, I say!— One: two: why, then 'tis time to do 't.— Hell is murky!— Fie, my lord, fie! a soldier, and afeared? What need we fear . . . ?' "

The voice that spoke behind her was not from the play. It was Aunt Judith's voice, cold with shock.

"Laura! What are you doing? What vile language are you using? I'd forgotten the wine jelly, so I returned. To find you— Your hair, Laura! Explain this matter to me at once."

Lauré turned, flushing scarlet. "I was rehearsing a scene from *Macbeth*," she said.

Judith Allen was not very tall, but she managed to give an impression of height with her ramrod stiffness of carriage, with the way she tilted her long nose and pinched in the thin nostrils. She seemed to grow in stature, and she gave the effect of smelling something very unpleasant indeed.

"Rehearsing? Rehearsing for what? That is a word of the stage, Laura, and you know I will have nothing of the stage in this house. When your father next returns to New York we must have this matter out once and for all."

Lauré did not permit a smile to reach her lips. As she suspected, Aunt Judith did not know that Jules Beaudine had brought his company back to New York two days ago, that it was already playing *Hamlet* at the Garrick Theater. If her aunt did not know, then there was the possibility that Lauré might reach him before Aunt Judith knew he was in town. Her father was always busy when he first reached New York. He would not come to see them right away.

"You've not answered me, Laura," Aunt Judith said, clasping her hands sternly before her and fixing her niece with her cold, sharp gaze.

"My name is Lauré," the girl said with spirit, though she knew the protest would do her no good.

"Lauré, Lauré! You know I will not use that ridiculous foreign name. Come now, answer me— What is it that you rehearse for? What foolish notions are you harboring? I'd thought all this was cured long ago."

"It will never be cured," Lauré said steadily. "Someday I will be an actress. Someday I will be on the stage with my father."

Aunt Judith moved decisively. She untied the strings of her bonnet and pulled it from her head, smoothed down sparse gray strands of hair, and moved firmly toward the door.

"Come with me," she said, and went out of the parlor and down the hall to the small, warm sitting room in the rear of the house.

Lauré took a moment to pin back her hair, so she would look less like a helpless child. Then she picked up the book of plays and followed her aunt reluctantly. The old trembling had begun at the pit of her stomach—the trembling that always came when she tried to pit her own young forces against Aunt Judith's steel and granite.

The furniture in the sitting room was old and nondescript. There was nothing here daylight could hurt, so the draperies were left open, though no light could brighten the dull browns and dark, forbidding maroons. Only the small fire on the hearth and the round-faced clock ticking on the mantel seemed alive and independent of Judith Allen's dour touch.

Her aunt thrust off her mantle, hung it carefully over the back of a chair, and seated herself primly in the rocker before the fire.

"Sit down," she told Lauré, motioning to a straight chair opposite. "I wish to talk to you."

Lauré took the chair and stared at the fire. She could not bear to look at her aunt lest futile tears start and reduce her entirely to the status of a child. She was no child, no matter what Aunt Judith and her father thought. Eighteen was a woman's age, and it was time she had some say in the arrangement of her own life.

"Your mother, Laura," Aunt Judith said, "was my young sister. She was the dearest being in the world to me. Since I was ten years older than she, when our mother died and later our father it was I who mothered her and raised her. I wanted no other family, no other home than the one I could make for Mary. I gave up everything for my little sister."

Lauré, staring at the fire, thought rebelliously that no one had a right to claim another so completely through self-sacrifice. She had heard this tale of the way her aunt had raised young Mary Allen so many times that she knew it by heart. But now Aunt Judith took the story along a new path, and Lauré's attention was suddenly arrested.

"I have never told you of the time when she ran away to marry your father," Aunt Judith said. "This has been a matter too painful for me to discuss. But now you should know the truth. Your mother had no talent for the stage, though she became an actress. Your father put a spell upon her—as he has put a spell upon the foolish women of this country for years. She went wherever he beckoned, did whatever he asked. And died of it. She was miserably unhappy."

Inside Lauré the knot of rebellion tightened. She knew none of the details of this runaway marriage, but she knew something else.

"That's not true!" she cried, and looked her aunt directly in the face. "It's not true that she was unhappy. That's a story you've told yourself until you believe it. But I was seven when she died, and seven is old enough for remembering. I remember how happy we were—all three of us!"

Aunt Judith went on as though she had not spoken. "Mary died of her own foolish mistake in a little town where the company was stranded and your father had scarcely the money for a meal. Had she been home and under proper care, she would be alive now. When your father brought you to me, and then went off to his wayward life again, I vowed that I would raise you as my own child and would keep you from making the mistake your mother made. I have kept that vow. I mean to go on keeping it."

But you never loved me, Lauré thought. You took me out of duty to my mother, but you hated me because I looked like my father and was my father's child. She dared put none of this into words, however.

Her aunt's attention focused abruptly on the book in Lauré's hands. She reached for it and riffled through the pages with an air of repugnance, as though it were an evil thing.

"I have forbidden you to have such books," her aunt said. "Where did you get this?"

"My father sent it to me last Christmas," Lauré said. "I asked him for it."

Aunt Judith flipped to the flyleaf where the bold scrawl of Jules Beaudine's signature was visible: "With love to my daughter."

"I will take care of this," she said.

"No!" Lauré cried, jumping up. "It's mine and you shan't take it!"

Her aunt rose from the rocker with dignity. "You will not speak to me in such a tone," she said. "Go to your room, Laura, and close the door. You are to stay there for the rest of the day, and I hope you will pray to the good Lord to save you from your wicked thoughts and words. There will be no more talk of rehearsing in this house. There will be no more reading of plays, or thinking of plays. Do I make myself clear?"

Old habit, old fear, was too strong. Hating herself for the weakness of giving in, Lauré made a quick curtsy as if she were indeed a child and went out of the sitting room. Then rebellion broke through again, and she ran angrily upstairs. She did not quite dare to bang the door of her room— banged doors had put her on a bread and milk diet more than once in the past. But she closed it more firmly than was necessary.

In her own room she minced primly across the floor in mimicry of Aunt Judith, satisfying something of her urge to strike back at her aunt through the rude portrayal. She only wished there were an audience present to see her. Always she had been able to send her friends into stitches with her imitations—further proof of her talent as an actress.

Now, however, the mimicry did not relieve her misery, and she flung herself upon the lumpy mattress of her small iron bed. In Aunt Judith's house one did not pamper oneself with beauty and comfort.

Her fingernails made red crescents in her palms and she bit her lips until the pain made her stop. She would not cry! She would be a baby no longer. Somehow she would find a way to escape from her prison. For a moment tears burned behind her eyes at the thought of her father's gift being confiscated, but she blinked them impatiently away. The book did not matter—except that she cherished all gifts from her father. But there were always volumes of Shakespeare to be purchased. The scenes were there in her head anyway—so many of them, all memorized, and played over and over in secret. Whispered to herself sometimes when she lay in bed at night, and sometimes acted out when her aunt was away from the house and she dared speak the lines aloud.

From Kate in *The Taming of the Shrew* to Portia and Lady Macbeth, she knew them. Not Cordelia or Juliet or Ophelia, with all of whom she felt some impatience. She liked Shakespeare's strong, willful, determined women better than she liked the sweet, gentle ones. Because *she* was like them, she told herself. Kate, the rebel, pleased her mightily. Kate would hurl Aunt Judith's words back in her teeth. Kate would stand up and fight. The part of the play Lauré liked least was toward the end when Katharine gave in to her lord Petruchio and turned so meek that she put her hands "below her husband's foot." She had never troubled to memorize the last scenes of the play after Kate had been tamed.

Thinking about Kate helped her courage. She rose from the bed and went to the door, listening tensely. Sometimes she could hear Aunt Judith's heavy breathing just beyond the panel, as her aunt tried to tell what she was doing.

But now the hall beyond Lauré's door was still. Quietly

she tilted a straight chair beneath the knob, so that the door could not be suddenly opened. Then she knelt beside her bed and pulled out a small chest, unlocking it with a key she kept on a chain about her neck.

With gentle, loving fingers she touched the few things hidden there. She studied the faded photograph of her mother—a girl's face, with curly blond bangs across the forehead and the sweetest of smiles on her lips. How pretty and young she had been! There was no doubting the happiness in her face.

In the chest was a handkerchief that had been her mother's, with handmade lace edging it, and a tiny Juliet cap sewed with seed pearls. Her father had given her the cap sadly one rare Christmas when he had been home and free to spend a little time with his daughter.

"She was not a very good Juliet," he told her. "But she was a lovely one and so sweet the audiences adored her, even if she spoke the lines stiffly. Perhaps you'd like to keep the cap she wore in the part. I came across it the other day when I was going through an old trunk."

Once more Lauré dipped into the chest and took out a sad Harlequin mask, crumpled around the edges, with its strings badly frayed. The mask had belonged to her father, and he had worn it for Mardi Gras in New Orleans in the long-ago boyhood he never spoke about.

She had always been curious about that part of his life, since it was the part he closed a door upon. Sometimes he would talk about New Orleans, but not about his life there. She knew only that he had grown up in a good Creole family and that he had caused a terrible scandal when he had decided as a very young man that he would go on the stage. Certain dignified professions were considered suitable for Creole gentlemen. For all that New Orleans was devoted to the theater, the profession of acting was not one of them. His father, Claude Beaudine, a well-known New Orleans lawyer, had set his heart on having his son follow in his steps and become an attorney. When Jules chose the stage instead, he had disowned his youngest son dramatically and finally. His mother, 'Toinette, had returned his letters unopened, as his father must have instructed her to do. For Jules Beaudine, on his way up in the theatrical firmament, the New Orleans life was ended and done with. He would not talk about it.

He had gone back only once, and then he had taken his wife with him in time for Lauré's birth. That seemed the strangest thing of all to Lauré—that she had been born in faraway New Orleans. Yet her parents had not stayed there long, and she had never learned what had transpired during that visit.

How he felt about New Orleans now, she did not know her father well enough to guess. The mask had been lent her for a child's party one time and he had never wanted it returned. Yet he had given his daughter a good French name, and Lauré often wondered how much of his family might remain in New Orleans, and what they were to her. Secretly, for Aunt Judith did not approve of any mention of the place of Lauré's birth, she had read what she could about the Crescent City on the Mississippi, and she had grown enormously curious about it.

There was a picture of her father in the chest too. She drew it out and studied the handsome, cleanly chiseled profile. There were silly women who fawned over him and said that he was the best-looking man in America. His daughter found it easy to agree that this must surely be true. She herself had inherited his dark Creole eyes and the mouth that was full and a little soft for a man. Her fair hair was her mother's, and her nose, as far as she knew, was her own. Yet, over-all, there was the look of her father in Lauré's face.

How little she knew him, really! It was not that he had ever seemed unloving. When he was with her he was given to an easy affection that she turned toward hungrily. But he was absorbed by his work and always busy. Even when he played in New York she did not see him often. Aunt Judith had forbidden her to go to any of his plays, or even to dine out with him, and her father, all too easily swayed by her strong-willed aunt, had agreed that the theater was no place for an impressionable young girl. So she had seen him on the stage only once.

When she was eleven she had run away to sit in a high balcony and watch his Brutus in *Julius Caesar.* How she had thrilled and wept and been carried away! Not even the switching Aunt Judith had given her later had made her tell where she had really been.

Another packet in the chest contained the letters her father had written her over the years. He did not write often, or at length, but he wrote well and there were always loving phrases to be found in the lines he sent her. Phrases she treasured and read over again and again. But even when she was quite young she had sensed that when he wrote he played the role of a father writing to a beloved daughter just as he played the father role when he visited her. She could never be sure what the man behind the written and spoken lines was really like.

All she had to guide her was the still-vivid memory of seven years of happiness and love and laughter, when life had been a delicious adventure, even though money was scarce, lodgings were cold, and theaters dingy firetraps. Someday she would have all that again—when she herself was an actress. Though when she had tried to tell her father her dreams, he smiled and said that all girls were stage-struck at one time or another, and she would outgrow such nonsense. She did not dare to tell him that she knew the role of Lady Macbeth by heart. She could imagine his laughter. His letters had scarcely changed over the years; he still wrote to her as if she were about nine years old, and sometimes she thought he had never truly realized that she was growing up.

Her fingers moved among old playbills, among a few ribbons, an envelope of pressed rose leaves from a bouquet her father had brought her. Then she put everything firmly back and locked the chest. The solution to her problem did not lie among souvenirs of the past. It lay in the hands of her father right now in the present. If she waited until he came to this house, it would be too late. Aunt Judith would reach him first and prejudice him with a relating of all his daughter's wrongdoings. He would never listen to her here. But if she went to him outside—!

Her breathing quickened at the thought. Today was Saturday—he would be playing a matinee. In fact, the play was on this very moment. If she went to the theater at once, she might be able to see him after the final curtain, catch him before he left for his lodgings. And why not? She was the daughter of Jules Beaudine and she surely had a right to see her own father.

By now Aunt Judith had probably taken the wine jelly and gone off again upon her visit, confident that her niece was repenting of her offense.

Lauré dressed quickly in her gray broadcloth winter suit and coat, and put on the gray hat with the white feathers on the brim. It was not as fashionable a costume as she would have wished, but Aunt Judith did not approve of fashionable styles. And at least she had the little gray squirrel muff her father had sent her to carry. With a bunch of imitation violets pinned to it, she could look fairly gay.

When she had assured herself that her aunt was no longer in the house, she went boldly down the stairs and out the front door. The February wind nipped at her cheeks, but her bright color was not due wholly to the cold as she turned west and began to walk briskly along the snowy street.

2. Backstage

SHE had not foreseen the trouble she might have at the stage door. The wizened little man who guarded that august portal sat with his chair tilted back. He frowned at her as she hurried up the steps and in out of the cold.

For a moment she hardly saw him as she stood blinking in a dim backstage world that brought memory flooding through her in a surprising tide. So much of this had been forgotten—or so she had thought. Yet here it was, familiar and recognizable: the bare wooden floor, scarred and not overly clean, the props and bits of scenery standing about, the vaulted darkness high overhead where curtains and flats hung out of the way—a world of rope and canvas. And toward the center of the area a glow of concentrated light, the murmur of voices that could mean only one thing—the stage.

The doorman lowered his chair to the floor and stood up. "What do you want, Miss?"

Lauré started and really looked at him for the first time. "Why," she faltered, "I—I just want to come in."

"You have a pass?" he asked.

"No—but I'm his daughter," she protested. "I'm Jules Beaudine's daughter."

The doorman grinned. "And I'm Queen Victoria's papa—that's who I am. Better be about your business now. You can't come in here."

She turned on him indignantly. "But I *am* Lauré Beaudine, and my father will be very angry if you don't let me in." She was not at all sure that was true, but it was the only argument she could think of. Anyway, she could tell by the doorman's face that it was no use. He didn't believe her and he didn't mean to let her in.

Rescue came from an unexpected quarter. A woman with her red hair piled high had paused near the door to listen. Suddenly she intervened.

"Let her in, Joe," she told the doorman. "The girl is Jules Beaudine's daughter, all right. Can't you see it in her face? Even with all that yellow hair, she's still got Jules's look about her."

The doorman flung up his hands. "Have it your way, Miss Tisdale. But you don't know how many chits like this one try to crash my door. If you say so, it's your responsibility."

He sat down again and tipped his chair back. The red-haired Miss Tisdale beckoned to Lauré.

"You may be fooling us, but I'll take a chance. Come

along and give Jules a surprise. He's been in a vile temper ever since we opened. Maybe you can cheer him up."

The state of her father's temper didn't sound promising, but Lauré had no intention of retreating now. As she followed Miss Tisdale, the very odors of backstage rose up from the past to engulf her in a nostalgia that made her ache with a strange longing. Scents of wood and dust, turpentine and grease paint drifted out of the past to mingle with the present and seemed as aromatic as the scent of a rose garden. Somehow it was the door of a happy time, long dead. This hushed, dim world was her world. This was where she belonged.

She could hear the voices from the stage more clearly now—in particular a deep ringing voice that was unforgettable—her father's voice.

" 'Sir, I will walk here in the hall: if it please his majesty, 'tis the breathing time of day with me; let the foils be brought, the gentleman willing, and the king hold his purpose, I will win for him an I can; if not, I will gain nothing but my shame and the odd hits.' "

Her heart beat a little faster at the words. That was Hamlet speaking before the duel with Laertes. It was nearly the end of the play.

The red-haired woman paused before a dingy door, which was no more distinguished than any other, except for the star painted upon its surface. It stood ajar and she looked in cautiously.

"His dresser's out for the moment—run in, dear, and make yourself at home." She smiled and turned to go, but something in Lauré's expression must have caught her eye. "Stand up to him," she whispered. "He has no patience with anyone he can frighten."

She closed the door and Lauré stood alone in her father's dressing room. Again a sense of the familiar possessed her. There were costumes hung on a rack, a wig flung upon a chair. Along one side of the bare, small room stretched a make-up shelf with a wide mirror above it. Pictures hung upon the walls—all of her father in roles he had played. There was Jules Beaudine as the mad Lear, with twigs and leaves in his hair. There was the young and handsome Hamlet, the troubled Brutus, the angry Moor, Othello. But she had no time now to study the pictures, fascinating though they might be.

Softly she moved to the mirror and gave herself a quick, uneasy glance. How red her cheeks were from cold and excitement, how pale her hair looked in the bright light over the make-up shelf! It was true that she was far from pretty—her father would never be pleased with her.

She noted objects upon the shelf with a further sense of recognition. Little pasteboard boxes of rouge, a rabbit's foot, powder-stained, a soft black eyebrow pencil, big tins of theatrical cream. Then a sound at the door startled her, and she sprang across the room, to stand half sheltered in the shadow of a black cape that hung from a coat tree.

The man who came in must be her father's dresser. He moved with middle-aged competence, picking up the wig from the chair, setting out a pair of slippers, brushing a dressing gown free of powder, not seeing her there in the corner of the room. She held her breath and made herself as small as possible. If he spied her, he might well put her out, as the man at the door had wanted to do.

She could hear the applause now, ringing through the theater. What a heady sound the clapping seemed to Lauré. How wonderful it would be to stand before footlights, bowing to that applause, accepting love and approval and adulation from all those you had held entranced through the magic of your acting!

The dresser went to the open door. He too was listening, but Lauré, peering out at him, saw him shake his head as if something was wrong. "Curtain's down too soon. Not near enough calls," he muttered and stepped back from the doorway.

Jules Beaudine came into the small dressing room like a thunderstorm, and there was no longer any hush backstage. It was fortunate that the audience filing out could not hear the star's displeasure.

"The house is half filled!" Jules cried, standing before his mirror in Hamlet's dark doublet and hose, studying himself with stormy eyes.

Lauré dared hesitate no longer. However much she might wish herself away, with her father in this mood, she was here and she must face what had to be faced. She stepped out behind him and he saw her there in the mirror. He looked neither more nor less angry, but merely stared at her, waiting.

His dresser saw her then and moved in her direction with an indignant gasp. Hamlet, still facing the mirror, his dark brows furrowed, put out his hand.

"Let be," he said. Then to Lauré: "Who are you? What do you want?"

In astonishment she returned his look in the mirror. It had never occurred to her that seeing her unexpectedly out of her own environment, dressed up in the garments of a young lady, her father might not recognize her. With a quick gesture she removed the hatpins from the big gray hat and took it off so that he could better see her hair.

"I'm Lauré," she said. "I had to see you, Father. I had to come!"

The lines in his face relaxed and suddenly he laughed, sounding no little embarrassed. He turned from the mirror and held out his arms to her in the proper gesture of a father who has not seen a beloved daughter for a long while. But even as she went into them she wondered what he truly felt at seeing her here. She let herself be held for a moment and kissed lightly on the cheek. But only when his hand strayed to touch her hair did she sense real emotion in him, and then she knew he was thinking of her mother.

He held her off at arm's length. "Forgive me, Lauré," he said. "Things have been going badly since we opened, and my mind was on other matters. To see you so unexpectedly, when only this morning I was remembering you as a child—well—"

"It's all right, Father," she told him. Close up like this, with the grease paint on his face, he did not look altogether familiar to her either. "I had to come," she repeated. "I had to see you away from Aunt Judith."

He ran a hand through thick dark hair that he allowed to grow wavy and long. "What's troubling Judith?"

Lauré faced him squarely. "It's just that I can't live with her any more. Living in her house is like living in a prison. I'm grown up now and I want to begin leading my own life."

It was the wrong moment to tell him this. She knew by the way he drew down his brows, by the angry twist to his mouth, but the words could not be withdrawn and she stood her ground.

"As though I hadn't enough troubles at the moment!" he cried. "Of course any change is impossible. You should know better than to come troubling me at the theater." Then he broke off and threw an apologetic look at his dresser, while something of his bluster died away. "I can see that the perils of fatherhood are about to descend upon me," he went on more moderately. "Whether I can deal with them or not, I don't know. At least, Daughter, give me leave to get out of this paint and padding. I suppose we must talk about this. If you'll wait for me, I won't be long. Then perhaps you'll have an early supper with me—I've another performance tonight—and we'll get to the bottom of this matter."

"Yes, of course, Father," she said, and went quickly out of the room.

Now she felt elated. In spite of his outburst, he had not said she must go straight home to Aunt Judith. He had not dismissed her as a foolish child. Indeed, she had seen in his eyes a surprised recognition of her as a young woman, and this boded well for her plans. Somehow, during the coming supper, she must convince him of the sincerity of her desire to go on the stage.

She went out of the dressing room to wait for him backstage. Once the curtain had been rung down, this was a different world. Some of the hush and the mystery were gone. People walked about freely, the scenery movers were at work. A stage manager was talking to one of the actors, still in costume. Lauré stepped unheeded into the wings, and as she stood there the curtain went up again upon an empty theater. Now the footlights were off, the house lights on, and she could look out upon the brown rows of seats, empty and program-littered, up to the boxes and the gilded curve of the high balconies.

This was a part of the theater she hardly knew. A few times as a child she had walked on in some small role, when a stage child was ill. She could just remember the look of faces out there beyond the bright footlights, the movement of hands clapping, the sound of approving laughter. This was the part she wanted to know better: to know in the role of Kate, perhaps, storming about a stage, astonishing an audience with her skill as an actress until applause would ring in actuality in her ears.

So lost was she in dreams that she did not note her father's presence until his hand touched her arm.

"You've that stage-struck look on your face," he said.

She turned toward him boldly. "Why shouldn't I have? I'm your daughter, and there's never been anything else I've wanted except to be with you, acting on the stage."

"Ridiculous!" he said, sounding cross again. "You haven't the faintest notion of what being an actor is like. Or what a frustrating, infuriating profession this can be. Come along—I'll feel better for some food. But I warn you, I don't mean to listen to talk of your going on the stage."

She went with him meekly past the doorman, who touched a finger to his forelock as Jules Beaudine went by. They took a hackney cab to Delmonico's, and Lauré shivered in secret delight as they walked into the famous dining room. Never would Aunt Judith be seen in a public dining room, least of all one frequented by actors. Lauré was sure her aunt would find something sinful in the very thought. She went in proudly on her father's arm and knew that the eyes of the room were upon them. It was a delicious feeling to know that other diners were probably wondering about the identity of the lady with golden hair in the company of Jules Beaudine. She decided to play her role to the hilt, and she moved with such dignity and hauteur that her father glanced at her in embarrassed surprise.

"This isn't the time or place to play Sarah Bernhardt," he murmured as he seated her at their table.

For a moment she felt deflated. Then she saw that he was smiling, and she gave up her play-acting to laugh cheerfully at herself. He laughed with her, and for a moment it was like long-ago remembered times.

It was more fun to be herself anyway—Cinderella at the ball. She had never imagined so large and elaborate a menu, with so much of it in French, and her eyes moved from one item to the next in happy bewilderment. Her father saw her predicament and ordered for her, so that she could relax and look eagerly about the room.

How beautiful it was, with all the gold and maroon and tall mirrors, the glitter of chandeliers! And how dignified the headwaiter looked! He had frightened her a little when they came in.

"How has your season been?" she asked her father politely. His few letters had been unusually short lately. Without make-up and the flattery of footlights, he looked like an older Hamlet, enormously handsome, somber of eye and brow, sober of mouth as befitted that solemn Dane.

"The season has been foul," he said flatly. "There's been a dearth of money everywhere, and people aren't turning out for the theater as they used to do. What's more, that loutish audience this afternoon sat on its hands and dared me to make it applaud. It was less a play than a duel between us." He brushed a hand across his brow. "I'm getting old and weary, I think."

That was foolish, of course, and she said so. There was not a line in his face, not a gray hair in the rich, dark brown sweeping back from his broad forehead.

He smiled a little sadly. "I have an eighteen-year-old daughter—something I've hardly realized until just this moment. I can't be very young, my dear."

The supper came and it was more elaborate and rich than Lauré would have wished, but she sensed that her father was trying to give her a special treat.

Over the superb turtle soup—something Lauré had never so much as tasted before—he talked on about his dissatisfaction with the theater. He was losing his leading lady shortly, among other difficulties. She was marrying and would leave the stage. Where he was going to find another young woman so talented, he had no idea. And at the moment, he felt too tired to search.

"You could try me," Lauré said, popping the words out before she could think and choke them back.

His laughter was hardly flattering, and she felt her cheeks burn at the sound of it. But she faced him stubbornly and did not smile.

"I know I'm not trained. That's your fault. If only you'd believed me, I could be ready now to go into your company. But even if I'm not ready for leading roles, I could play bits. You don't know how hard I've worked!"

"Worked?" he said, staring at her.

"Memorizing practically whole plays of Shakespeare, playing some of the women's parts over and over at home before a mirror."

"I suppose you think that qualifies you for the professional stage?" he asked mockingly. "And what does your Aunt Judith say about all this?"

"That's why I'm here," she told him quickly. "She caught me at it today and she took away the book of plays you gave me last Christmas. She said she would have nothing of the theater in her house. But the thing neither of you seems to realize is that I was practically born in the theater. I belong there. Truly I do, Father."

He sighed. "Your aunt is right. The theater is no place for a woman."

He returned her look with so much unhappiness in his eyes that she was startled. She had thought of him always as a man at the peak of his career, successful, sought after, sure of himself in every way. But now he was studying her with an air of confusion and sadness, as though he did not know what to do about her, or how to meet the words she had hurled at him.

"Your mother did not belong in the theater," he said. "I can never forget that."

"That's not true!" Lauré cried. "My mother loved the theater."

Gently he shook his head. "Your mother loved me, not the theater. I will not have you make her mistake. Every young girl is stage-struck and—"

"You always say that," she protested. "If only you'd give me a chance to show you what I can do! If you'd let me read to you, recite!"

Her father recovered himself at that, the look of uncertainty gone from his eyes. He paid no attention to the waiter taking away their plates, but struck one hand dramatically to his forehead in a gesture of despair. "Preserve me from young ladies who recite! Spare me that, Daughter, please."

She fell silent, helpless. How was she ever to convince him when he refused to so much as listen to her read a scene from a play?

"I will not go back to Aunt Judith's," she said at last, and her voice, though faint, did not quaver.

The waiter brought their next course, but as they ate, Lauré's words seemed to hang in the air between them, barring all other conversation. When she had begun to think he would never speak to her again, he reached suddenly across the table for her hand and held it lightly in his own slender, expressive fingers.

"Very well then, my dear. You shall not go back for the time being. You shall come with me."

Joy leaped into her eyes. Had she been younger she would have run around the table to hug him ecstatically. "Oh, Father!" she murmured, out of breath with delight.

But there was no laughter in his eyes as he answered her. "You shall come with me, Lauré. But not on the stage. I'm going to close the company shortly and go to New Orleans for a holiday. If you like, you may accompany me there."

3. Garden District

LAURÉ'S first reaction was one of disappointment, indeed of rebellion. A holiday in a strange Southern city—even one she was curious about—was the last thing she wanted. But good sense restrained her, and she managed to keep her feelings to herself.

"You always said you would never go back to New Orleans," she remarked wonderingly. "You said you'd never go near your family until they sent for you."

"I've no intention of breaking my word." He sounded curt. "I shall probably not go near the Vieux Carré, the French Quarter, where I was born. Foster Drummond, a chap I went to school with, has a home in the Garden District. He and his wife have been after me to come down for a visit, and I've accepted. The season is going badly and I need a rest."

She asked her next question a little timidly. "Are your mother and father living?" It was as if she spoke of strangers who had no connection with her. Except for Aunt Judith, there was no family left on her mother's side, and she was not accustomed to the thought of grandparents.

"My father died five years ago," he said. "Foster wrote me at the time. There has never been any communication from my mother. She always followed my father's lead in everything. It's unlikely that she'd open her door to me now, even if I stood at her gate. She must be nearly seventy. I was her youngest son."

What a bitter thing it must have been to be disowned by his parents after the quarrel with his father, refused the door of his own home! Lauré thought. He must have had courage to follow his own star in the face of such stern opposition. Perhaps it was because she was like him that she too could hold so unswervingly to a goal. His own experience ought to make him better able to understand her desire, but it didn't seem to have that effect.

He dropped lumps of sugar in his coffee cup and stirred thoughtfully. "I'm not sure I'd be doing a wise thing to take you along. I know nothing about the raising of daughters, and I might regret this step before I'm through."

"I'll give you no trouble," she assured him quickly.

He studied her across the table as if he was trying to understand exactly what she was like, to know her as he had never been able to before.

"I'm not sure about that," he said. "You have the look of trouble about you. The set of your chin, the look in your eyes—the whole effect is altogether too—disturbing."

Now she was curious. What did he see in her face? What did he mean?

"Why do you think I have a look of trouble about me?"

He countered with a question of his own. "How many young men of your own age do you know well?"

"Young men?" She stared at him, startled. What had men to do with this?

"You've heard of men, I suppose?" he asked dryly. "In spite of the fact that you've attended a very proper young lady's seminary? Or has your Aunt Judith kept you away from them entirely? You've grown up mainly in a woman's world, haven't you?"

She nodded wordlessly, breaking the crisp outer crust of the *meringue glacée* the waiter had set before her. Of course she had known some boys and men. Two or three, at least. There was the grocer's delivery boy who had come to the house all last year and to whom she had fancied she had lost her heart—though she'd spoken hardly more than a handful of words to him on extremely prosaic matters. That hadn't lasted, though. He was too indifferent.

Then there'd been the handsome young doctor who came briefly to treat her aunt's megrims while the senior doctor was away. He had looked at her with interest and he'd taken great trouble to explain the prescription he left behind. Aunt Judith had not approved of him. And there was her best friend's brother Henry—a great hulk of a fellow, who had caught her in the back hallway of his house once and kissed her soundly. She had never liked him. She had thought the experience unpleasant and she had slapped him hard. And yet—the incident had been exciting in a way, and she had gone on to weave impossible fantasies, changing him in her mind to all that he was not. Of course she wanted to meet men, and one special man she could know well. But it was impossible to confess to Jules Beaudine that the only men she really knew bore names like Petruchio, Romeo, Hamlet, and Lysander, and lived only in plays.

Again her father sighed in perplexity. "Some men are not born for parenthood. I'm one of them, and I suppose I've done my best to side-step some of its unpleasant aspects. It would be very nice having a daughter I need see only at her best and who would never be a burden or trouble to me. But perhaps I've worried a bit more about you than I've wanted to. Or than I let you know."

His smile lessened the hurt of his words. He was honest, at least. She had always known these things about him. It would be foolish to pretend he was a typical father such as other girls had.

"In taking you with me to New Orleans," he went on, "I'm breaking all the rules I've laid down for myself. But at least you will discover what an impossible father I am, and you'll get over your absurd notion that you want to act in my company."

She believed none of this but she was silent.

"I've met Celeste Drummond a few times when she came north with her husband," he went on. "Foster is no Creole, but she is, and I've no doubt that she is sensible about daughters, having one of her own. Perhaps she can give you a bit of the social life you've never had with your aunt, keeping you in line the while, of course."

"In line?" Lauré objected. "Father, I'm eighteen. There's no need—"

He shook a finger at her. "The Drummonds' daughter is only eight, but they also have a son who is past twenty—a boy they're having some difficulty with. If I bring you down there, you'll probably take one look at Cole Drummond and fall in love with him. I wonder if I should take that risk?"

"Oh, Father!" she protested. "I wouldn't be so ridiculous. Besides, I'm more grown up than you realize. Mother was a year younger than I when she married you."

He raised a silver spoon beside his plate and thudded it on the tablecloth, silencing her.

"That's it exactly. The same pattern your poor mother followed. She'd hardly talked to a man until I came along. I stole her right from under your aunt's nose, and because I was the first man she knew, she fell in love with me. She was too frail for stage life, too gentle for its rough ways. But if it hadn't been me, she'd have met someone else and the same thing would have happened. Now it's likely to happen to you. Instead of knowing any number of boys, which is normal for the young, you've now arrived at the place where you will take one look at some impossible young man and decide that he is for you. Probably the first one you're introduced to, since you have no measuring stick and will know no better."

How exasperating he could be! "Father, I'm not nearly so foolish as you think. Besides, I'm not pretty, as Mother was. Probably no young man will ever—"

"That has nothing to do with breaking your heart," he told her. "Pretty you're not. And sometimes, when you draw your mouth down like that, you're quite plain. But there's more in your face than mere prettiness. Something more distinctive. Dress you up properly, give you some poise and a happy expression, and you might pass for a beauty. And the illusion of beauty is much more dangerous than real prettiness, my dear. You'll make a man curious about you. He'll want to know what you're thinking, what you're really like, and that can lead to trouble."

She had to smile at him then. Such a strange, wonderful thing for him to say. After all the years in which Aunt Judith had sternly discounted her appearance, it made her feel more confident already.

His mood shifted, and he returned her smile. "Never mind—we'll take the risk. I'm sick of winter cold and gray skies. Lauré, the sun is out in New Orleans, and before long the camellias and azaleas will be blooming. We'll be in time for Carnival—for Mardi Gras—which comes in early March this year. You've never lived, daughter, until you've seen Carnival time in New Orleans. Finish your dessert, and then we'll go home and tell your aunt our plans. Though I must say I dread the idea. This isn't going to be easy, you know."

It proved to be even more difficult than they anticipated. When Lauré went home with her father, Aunt Judith was ready for them. She had lighted a fire in the seldom-used parlor and she sat waiting amidst her gilt and red-velvet treasures, as if the very dignity of this room gave her additional strength.

Jules Beaudine did his best to explain, adopting a manner that was a bit too jovial for the occasion. Aunt Judith paid little attention to him. She glanced at him once and said: "You are not on the stage now, Jules. We speak quietly in this house," and he subsided like a small boy. "Laura, you will explain, if you please," she directed.

It was clear to Lauré that she would have to do most of this herself. She could not altogether blame her father, knowing as she did how much he dreaded visiting Aunt Judith's cold, domestic world. He did not like to make himself uncomfortable in this particular way.

"I had to see my father," Lauré said, meeting her aunt's eyes without faltering. "Neither of you has recognized that I'm growing up and that I can't go on living here like an imprisoned child."

"You use an emotional term," Aunt Judith said tartly. "A well-brought-up young woman who terms herself a prisoner is being ridiculous."

"Nevertheless," said Lauré, clinging to her purpose, "I want to go away. Father is closing his company until fall and I am going with him to New Orleans."

Her aunt did not move at all, except to close her eyes for a moment. When she opened them, it was clear that her resolve had stiffened by another degree.

"I do not intend you to go to that wicked city," she said. "I shall not allow it. Put this plan out of your mind at once. She cannot go with you, Jules."

By now Jules was looking thoroughly uncomfortable, but

he made an attempt to aid his daughter. "After all, the choice is hers," he said mildly. "It's true that she is eighteen and able to make such decisions for herself."

"Like my poor sister, I suppose?" Aunt Judith cried. "No—I shan't allow it! I shall oppose this move to my last breath."

"Perhaps you don't understand." Jules's tone was gentle. "This is merely for a visit. We'll spend the idle season in New Orleans and then return north in the fall. What we plan next can be talked about later."

"If she goes, she will never come back," Aunt Judith said, and there was an unexpected sound of pain in her voice. Lauré glanced at her in surprise, but she went on at once. "Do you remember, Jules, when you took my little sister away that last time? I never saw her again. I can't endure to have that repeated."

Again Jules's voice was kind. "I haven't forgotten, Judith. I have no wish for Lauré to go on the stage. You were right in the unhappy things you prophesied for Mary. I promise you they won't be repeated."

Before the continued gentleness in his tone, Aunt Judith seemed to crumple into a betrayal of feeling that Lauré had never seen in her before. She watched in uneasy astonishment as Aunt Judith took a handkerchief from her sleeve and touched it to her reddening eyes.

"I've wanted only the best for Mary's daughter," she murmured. "I have given up my life to protecting her from—"

This was too much, and Lauré broke in vehemently. "You shouldn't have given your life! No one asked it of you. And you can't keep another person from living, through your sacrifice."

Her aunt looked at her sadly, without understanding. She seemed suddenly older than Lauré had realized—older and more helpless. The stern, iron-willed woman she remembered from her childhood was vanishing before her eyes. Why, I am stronger than she is, Lauré thought in dawning wonder. We've changed places, and she can't reach me any more. Awareness of her own strength gave her a new feeling of pity toward her aunt and a quick flash of understanding. Aunt Judith, by her own lights, had always done the right thing, and she would never see herself in any other way. Those who might see more clearly could afford to be kind.

Jules had risen somewhat restlessly, and Lauré turned to him quickly. "I know you must get back to the theater, Father. Let me know when your plans are made. I can be ready to leave whenever you want me."

She went with him to the door and he put an arm about her. The brief moment was one of affection between them, and she suspected that he understood a great deal more about Aunt Judith than she had realized. She watched him go off down the street with a sense of having grown up a little in her own perceptions.

When she returned to the parlor, the lamps had been extinguished and the fire was dying. The room was an empty shell, and somehow no longer the formidable place she remembered. She went softly up to her own room and began to lay her clothes upon the bed, sorting out things that might be suitable for her trip, laying aside garments that needed mending.

A half hour later her aunt came into the room and sat down beside her to watch. All trace of emotion was gone from her face, and it was clear that she intended a new attack. Lauré found that she could smile at her without rancor.

"They'll snub you, you know," Aunt Judith began without preamble. "That's what those stiff-necked Creoles did to your mother when your father took her there in time for your birth. I never could understand why he made such a to-do about having you born in New Orleans—when his parents wouldn't speak to him, or look at his wife, much less at his daughter. His father never forgave him for having a mind of his own. Besides, Creoles think they are better than anyone else. You won't like being snubbed."

"I am half Creole," Lauré said. "It's time I found out about that part of my family."

Her aunt picked up a shirtwaist with a missing button and threaded a needle. Now and then she made some remark against the trip, but the heart seemed to have gone out of her arguments. For the rest of the evening they worked together almost companionably.

In the next few days Lauré had a great deal to think about. This matter of being a Creole, for instance. Not that Foster Drummond was Creole. He was an "American," as the Creoles used to call the outsiders when they first came to Louisiana. Her father had explained the word "Creole" to her long ago when she had asked him questions.

New Orleans had known many flags. It had been French, then Spanish, then French again, and finally American. In the beginning the French and Spanish had hated each other, but in the end their blood and customs had mingled, and children born in New Orleans of those early settlers were known as "Creoles." Predominantly the culture was French, but many touches of the Spanish remained, particularly in the architecture of the Vieux Carré—the Old Square of original New Orleans. It was there the Beaudine house still stood on Royal Street.

The Garden District, her father had explained, was the beautiful residential section the Americans had built above Canal Street when the Creoles would not accept them. Many wealthy families lived there now, whereas the old Creole town had fallen into decay. Foster Drummond was president of a bank and very well to do, but he had never forgotten his friend Jules, and once or twice in the past when things had gone badly he had even offered a loan. Now that Jules Beaudine was an impressive success, he would welcome the chance to entertain him in his own home. Lauré gathered that her father would take a certain pleasure in lording it in New Orleans, after the way the city of his birth had treated him in the past.

"How long will we stay?" Lauré had asked.

Her father only shrugged. "Who knows? In New Orleans a visit can last months. We'll be welcome as long as we wish to remain. I mean to forget the theater for a while and renew myself in surroundings I like."

But Lauré knew that she would not forget the theater. She would seize this opportunity to know her father better, and sooner or later she would find a way to impress him with her ability, wear down his objection to her going on the stage. If she chafed a little at the delay, she accepted it as necessary and was able to prepare for the trip with eager excitement. She packed a few mementos to take with her. Her mother's picture, for one thing, and, for sentimental reasons, the little Juliet cap. Who could tell—someday she might wear it on a stage. She must keep it always with her for luck.

When she said good-by to Aunt Judith, she was more moved that she expected. This was a step into the future and away from the past, and they both knew it.

"You will remember the things I have taught you, Laura?" Aunt Judith said.

"I will remember," Lauré assured her, and knew very well that she would.

She put her arms about her aunt and kissed her cheek lightly. Was it possible, she thought, that there were tears in her aunt's eyes as she and her father went out of the house?

When their train left New York that day, a February blizzard sheathed the city in ice and snow, but as they moved south the sun came out and the air grew warmer.

Jules Beaudine was recognized on the train, of course, and while he seemed casual about the matter, Lauré suspected that any recognition of his fame gratified him and that he would have been troubled if no one had known who he was. The role of famous actor was second nature to him, and he played it grandly. Nor did he hesitate to make his displeasure felt when matters did not run according to his standards. There was an occasion or two when Lauré was distinctly embarrassed. Her father had a temper he was quite willing to display when the occasion arose.

But at length the long, grimy trip was behind them. Mr. Drummond was out of town on business, but a carriage was sent to meet their train. As they drove through the city in a victoria, Lauré looked with pleasure upon the lawns and gracious homes of the Garden District. How different from the cold stone vistas of New York!

As the carriage pulled up before the house on St. Charles

Avenue, Mrs. Drummond came out to the steps to welcome them. The big white house had a wide lower gallery around two sides, and an upper one above. Slender white columns of the Greek revival period marched across the front. The upper gallery was intricately trimmed in iron grillwork, after the Spanish manner. An iron fence ran along the front of the property, and there was a marble carriage block at the curb.

Celeste Drummond was a strikingly handsome woman with the full figure that was fashionable near the end of the century. She wore an afternoon frock of pale yellow, and her dark hair was piled in a high pompadour style. Her brilliant dark eyes glowed with the warmth of her welcome.

"Foster is devastated that he couldn't be here to greet you," she said, holding both hands out to Jules and accepting his kiss upon her cheek. Then she turned with equal friendliness to Lauré. "So you are the little one Jules has written us about? But not so little any more, I should say. You are very welcome, my dear."

Her openhearted greeting seemed a little overwhelming after Aunt Judith's bleak manner. Lauré found that she could not behave in an equally uninhibited way. Her father fell into the role easily and comfortably—but then, he had grown up in New Orleans.

As Mrs. Drummond led the way into the wide hallway with its dark, polished floor and gracefully curving staircase, a little girl came rushing into the hall, a schoolbag of books banging against her knees. She had clearly been running and was out of breath. She flung herself upon her mother with an air of entreaty and Mrs. Drummond smiled and turned her about to face the guests.

"This is my daughter, Jessamyn, and I suspect that she has

run all the way home from school to greet you. Jessamyn, this is Mr. Beaudine, and this is his daughter, Lauré."

Jessamyn had long brown hair and bangs, and her mother's great dark eyes. She turned her rapt gaze first upon Jules and then upon Lauré and opened her mouth. Her mother, probably well versed in Jessamyn's eight-year-old curiosity, touched her gently on the shoulder.

"Not now, darling. Our guests are tired, I'm sure. You can save your questions till later."

Lauré smiled at the way the little girl closed her mouth as if she stemmed the tide with difficulty. The son, Cole, was not in evidence, and as they went upstairs Mrs. Drummond murmured that he was away and she didn't know when to expect him back in town. There was a sigh in her voice as she spoke of him, and Lauré found herself wondering what sort of escapade he was involved in that so troubled his family.

Jules Beaudine was shown into a large room, opening upon a side gallery, and he entered it dramatically. "I've come home!" he announced. "Camping out of a trunk as I do, I'd almost forgotten what gracious living is like. I don't know why I've stayed away so long."

Lauré's room was smaller and very charming, over-looking the garden at the rear. Blue cornflowers sprinkled the wallpaper, and the ruffled curtains at each window were starched and sparkling white. She couldn't resist bouncing on the bed at once, and found it soft as eider down could make it. Aunt Judith would certainly disapprove of all this pleasant comfort.

A Negro maid brought Lauré's portmanteau to her room, delivered a pitcher of hot water, and asked if there was anything she could do. Lauré thanked her and sent her away. She wanted only to be alone, to bathe, to rest a little and get used to these agreeable changes in her life. Everything had come so breathlessly fast that there had been no time to stop and savor along the way.

Jessamyn, however, still hovered in the doorway, eying her with interest. "You don't look like a famous actress," she said frankly.

Lauré's laughter rippled. "Whatever made you think I was? It's my father who is famous."

"But your mother was an actress too. Mamma said so. She said you were on the stage as a child, and it would be a miracle if it wasn't in your blood also. So why aren't you famous by now?"

Jessamyn was telling more than her mother would have wished, but Lauré did not mind these revelations. Indeed she was flattered to think that the Drummonds expected her to belong to the world of the theater.

"I was on the stage for only a little while, when I was younger than you are," Lauré said. "But I'll tell you a secret. Someday I *am* going to be a famous actress."

Jessamyn tilted her head to one side and studied Lauré thoughtfully. "I've seen lots of plays and actresses, but you don't look like any I've seen. You aren't—well, you aren't very beautiful."

"Jess-a-myn!" That was Celeste Drummond's voice, and the summons was loving, but imperative.

"I'm coming, Mamma," Jessamyn called back to her. Then she stuck her head into the room once more and whispered to Lauré in a conspiratorial voice. "You've set everyone on his ear by coming here, you know. Your cousin

Arcadie is wild with excitement, though she's been forbidden to speak to you. And I'll bet the aunts will be over next door the moment they get a chance, in order to peek at you and your father. I think there's going to be a lovely *scandale*."

She waved a cheerful hand and went off before Lauré, momentarily stunned, could recover and ask some questions of her own.

With the door closed behind Jessamyn, Lauré took off her hat and slipped out of the jacket that was too warm for February in New Orleans. As she began to bathe away the train grit, she tried to sort over the curious hodgepodge of information that had been hurled at her so suddenly.

She had aunts, and a cousin named Arcadie who was "wild with excitement." The feud apparently still held, because this cousin had been forbidden by someone to speak to her. By Jules's mother, she supposed. Her own grandmother. What was she like, Lauré wondered—that old lady close to seventy who was so hardhearted that she had not communicated with her son in more than twenty years?

Well—the answers would undoubtedly be forthcoming, and life in New Orleans promised to be far from dull, even though it postponed the appearance of Lauré Beaudine in the theater.

4. *The Aunts Retreat*

DURING the next day or so Lauré discovered that she had arrived in New Orleans at a time when the tempo was swift and exciting. Carnival was in the air, and she had to confess her ignorance of all that Carnival meant. She knew that there would be parades with floats, and that people went abroad masked and in costume, but she began to realize at once that she had not dreamed of the complications, the intricacy, or the ceremonies within ceremonies that keyed the entire city to a pitch of gaiety and fun-making in the days before Lent.

One morning two days after her arrival, she sat upon a slipper chair in a bright, spacious bedroom while a dressmaker knelt at Mrs. Drummond's feet, her mouth full of pins as she fitted a handsome ball gown of Nile green satin trimmed in black lace. This was Saturday, and Jessamyn was home from school. The little girl sat on a footstool near Lauré, with her hands clasped about her knees, watching her mother raptly.

"When I'm grown up I shall be a Carnival queen," she announced confidently.

Her mother's dark eyes sparkled with amusement. "My daughter is bound she will outdo me—since I was only a maid of honor as a girl."

The little dressmaker sounded shocked as she mumbled through the pins: "Only maid of honor, indeed! And in the court of the Twelfth-night Revelers, at that. A very *special* honor!"

"She still has her silver bean," Jessamyn said. "Mamma, may I show Lauré the bean?"

Mrs. Drummond nodded, laughing. "The Twelfth-night Revelers is the only krewe that chooses its queen and maids of honor with gold and silver beans. It was terribly exciting when the pieces of cake were given us, and no one knew which slices contained the gold bean that would designate the queen or the silver beans that chose the maids of honor."

Jessamyn ran to her mother's dressing table and came back with a small silver patch box. In a nest of cotton within was the little silver bean that Celeste Drummond had found in her slice of cake.

"Did that mean you rode on one of the floats in the parade?" Lauré asked.

Miss Willis nearly swallowed her pins, and even Mrs. Drummond looked faintly shocked.

"Dear me, no," she said. "No lady ever sets foot on a Carnival float. The floats belong to the secret societies, of which only men are members. There's the Krewe of Comus, the Knights of Momus, and of course the Krewe of Rex. Rex is king of all the Carnival. And there are others, besides. Every krewe chooses its own king and queen and maids of honor. But only the men of the court parade on the floats. The women sit in reviewing stands and receive their homage. And of course they dance at the balls."

"Mamma has already been to four balls this season," Jessamyn said proudly. "This dress is for her last one a few days before Mardi Gras."

Lauré returned the silver bean, her head spinning. Here was a world she knew nothing about and which everyone, including Miss Willis, seemed to take very seriously.

"I'm glad you are here in time to see something of the fun," Mrs. Drummond told her. "Though it's too bad you weren't here in time to be invited to a ball. There are only a limited number of invitations given out, and it's not easy to attend. We can probably get an invitation for your father, at least, since a few are always held for visiting celebrities. When I was a girl, I used to dance through an entire season, but now as a rule Foster and I go only as spectators."

"Cole has an invitation too," Jessamyn reminded her mother.

Celeste Drummond's eyes clouded. "He may not return to New Orleans in time," she said. "I'm terribly worried about him."

Lauré was curious about this missing son, but the subject was clearly an unhappy one for his mother and she made no attempt to pursue it.

"When do people dress up and wear masks?" she asked.

"That's on Mardi Gras—the last day of Carnival," Jessamyn said. "The name means Fat Tuesday."

"And does everyone mask and wear costumes?"

Once more it was clear that Lauré had said something a little shocking.

"Masking is for the *gens du commun*—the common people," Mrs. Drummond said. "Of course men may do as they please and many a gentleman masks. But it would not be suitable for a lady of good family. We prefer to hold our Carnival celebrations more decorously in private."

That seemed rather a pity, Lauré thought, though she did not say so. A day when the populace dressed up and pretended to be someone or something it was not, sounded like a good deal of fun.

Released from the hands of Miss Willis, Celeste Drummond moved regally before her long mirror, turning this way and that to see every fold of her gown.

"I think it will do nicely," she said and waved her hands at the girls. "The performance is over—you may run along now." And then, just as they reached the door, "Oh, Lauré—I meant to ask you—you've brought party dresses along, of course?"

Lauré thought of the modest frock which her aunt had considered her best dress. "I—I have only one," she said in embarrassment.

"A girl of eighteen who has brought just *one* party dress to New Orleans?" Mrs. Drummond cried. "That won't do at all. Miss Willis, do take Lauré's measurements while you have the chance. She must have at least one other frock as soon as possible. Lauré, you can wear the dress you have for the soirée, night after tomorrow. But we must be prepared for invitations after that. I'm sure your papa will want you to look your best."

"This is the busy season, Mrs. Drummond—" Miss Willis began.

"I know it is," Mrs. Drummond said cheerfully. "But I've seen you manage miracles before. And surely your work dies down a little toward the end of the season."

Miss Willis gave up and went to work with her tape measure.

"What is the party day after tomorrow?" Lauré asked, increasingly bewildered.

"It's just a small evening party we're giving for your father and you, my dear," Celeste Drummond said airily. "A few relations and close friends—no more than thirty or forty people. There's no big ball that night, and I think our guests will come. Of course the Creoles will be curious about Jules Beaudine and his daughter. After all, you're one of them." There was a note of affectionate understanding in her voice. As a Creole herself, she knew whereof she spoke.

Lauré stood still and straight while Miss Willis measured her a bit frantically, as if she had already begun to hurry on this unexpected assignment. When it was possible to escape, Lauré slipped away by herself to the side garden.

It was still winter in New Orleans, but not winter in the sense that Lauré knew it in New York. Today seemed a warm gift from the spring that still lay ahead, and she crossed the wide lawn to a small white summerhouse, glad to be outdoors. The sides of the summerhouse were open all around, so that she could see the street and the house next door across the lawn between.

It was quiet here, and she hoped that she could be alone for a little while. This desire, however, was quickly frustrated by Jessamyn, who had been determinedly looking for her. Lauré made room for the little girl on the bench beside her. Perhaps this might be an opportunity to learn more about the missing Cole.

"Has your brother been away long?" she asked tentatively.

Jessamyn stared at her as if she was trying to make up her mind whether to speak. Then she picked up the bait and was off with it.

"Not so long—but he's in terrible trouble. Everyone is upset about him."

"So I gathered," Lauré said and hoped Jessamyn would go on.

The child needed no prodding. Her eyes were aglow with excitement now. "Cole gambled a lot of money that was entrusted to him," she announced dramatically. "And he lost all of it. Then of course he was challenged to a duel."

Lauré looked at the child in dismay. "How dreadful! No wonder your mother is upset. But he won't really fight, will he? I mean, dueling must surely be against the law."

"Of course it is, but that wouldn't stop Cole. That's why

he's had to flee New Orleans."

"You mean—?"

Jessamyn nodded, her excitement rising. "They've already met under the Duelling Oaks in City Park. And the other man was seriously wounded. He's in the hospital, and if he dies—"

There were sudden tears in Jessamyn's eyes, and Lauré, shocked as she was, tried to console her. "Don't worry. He'll probably be all right. At least it's lucky that your brother wasn't hurt."

"He was only grazed," Jessamyn told her. "The doctor said the wound was nothing, if he would just take care of it. But you don't know Cole. Mamma says he has given her dozens of new gray hairs. That's why Papa is away—trying to take care of things and hush everything up. But Papa will be home tonight, I think. Don't let anyone know I've told you all this."

"I won't," Lauré promised. "Though I really think you shouldn't tell anyone else."

Jessamyn said: "I know. It's just that you're practically family. Of course if the other man dies, Cole would be a— a—" she lowered her voice to a frightened whisper, "a murderer. Have you ever known a murderer, Lauré?"

Lauré could only shake her head at so startling a question. The mystery behind Cole Drummond was more disturbing than she had imagined, and now she found herself more curious than ever about him. Checking back over the boys she had known, however slightly, she could not imagine one of them gambling recklessly, getting himself in debt, or—above all things!—fighting a duel.

All this, she supposed, was in keeping with New Orleans

history. The hot-tempered Creoles had been given to gambling and to dueling on the slightest pretext. Her father had told her that in the cemeteries here were many graves of those *"morts sur le champ d'honneur"*—dead on the field of honor. Cole was half Creole, so dueling was probably in his blood. Perhaps it wasn't fair that he should be considered a criminal because of this escapade, when this sort of thing must be a part of his immediate heritage.

Oh, dear! she thought, pulling her thoughts up short—here she was practically defending this dreadful young man. Dueling was wicked and justifiably outlawed. She was glad she wouldn't have to meet Cole Drummond. There was nothing about him of which she could approve, and she would not, of course, wish to know him. Having come to this sensible conclusion, she wondered why she should feel suddenly let down and disappointed.

Wheels sounded in the street just then, and the clop-clop of horses' hoofs as a carriage drew up next door. Jessamyn jumped up to see who was arriving. Then she squeezed Lauré's arm and whispered to her, Cole momentarily forgotten.

"There! What did I tell you? See the two old ladies getting out of the carriage, and the girl with them?"

A colored coachman sprang down to help the ladies. The two older ones stepped creakily out of the carriage, looking like identical paper dolls. Both were thin and dressed completely in black, from their high laced shoes to their ancient bonnets. But in spite of their dress, these two did not remind Lauré in the least of her Aunt Judith. For one thing, they were more twittery. They leaned on each other and sent darting little glances timidly about them, as if they thought they might see something they were afraid to see. The girl with them was young and very pretty—a little younger than Lauré, perhaps. She had glossy dark hair, a pert straight nose, and a lovely soft mouth with lips that parted now a little breathlessly.

She ran up the steps of the house next door ahead of her two elderly companions, and as she did so she looked straight toward the summerhouse and saw Lauré sitting there. Lively interest quickened in her face, though she gave no other sign that she had seen the two who watched her arrival. Her companions, twittering in French, climbed the steps more slowly, and they too glanced briefly in the direction of the summerhouse. They must have seen her, Lauré thought, for they reacted as if they had been burned, averting their faces at once. As they went up the steps, the black bonnets acted as blinders and cut off any further glimpse of something they clearly did not wish to see.

Jessamyn wriggled in delight. "I knew they'd come. Those two are your funny old Creole aunts. Your great-aunts, really—your grandmother's sisters. They're pretending they didn't see you, but when they're out of sight I bet they'll peek through the window at you. The girl is your cousin Arcadie. She's nice. I like Arcadie."

Lauré watched with interest until the door opened and all three went inside. "If she's my cousin, perhaps I could go next door and introduce myself. Perhaps she doesn't know who I am."

Jessamyn shook her head wisely. "She knows. That's why she's here. That's why the two aunts are here. But if you go over, the aunts won't speak to you and that won't be very nice. Just wait and leave it to Arcadie."

So they sat there in the summerhouse, enjoying the bright sunshine. A small green lizard came out and stared at them curiously before he flicked his tail and frisked out of sight.

The quiet was broken at length by the opening of a side door in the other house and the soft thud of feet hurrying down the steps. Lauré peered out to see the dark-haired girl running across the lawn from next door. She was laughing as she came, and she ducked hurriedly into the summer-house, shielding herself from view behind one of its vine-covered columns. When she had kissed Jessamyn on the cheek, she turned eagerly to Lauré and held out both hands. There was a flavor of French in her words as she spoke.

"You are my cousin from the North, *n'est-ce pas?* I am Arcadie Beaudine and I welcome you to New Orleans." She had such charm and gaiety, this pretty little cousin, that Lauré warmed to her at once. When she took Arcadie's hands to return the greeting, Arcadie at once pulled her face down and kissed each cheek. She smelled cleanly of something like orris root and violet sachet.

"You ran away from the aunts, didn't you?" Jessamyn said.

Arcadie rolled her eyes heavenward dramatically. "They are such dears and they do not fool anyone—them. As soon as word reached us that Jules Beaudine was returning to New Orleans and bringing his daughter to stay with the Drummonds, Tante Sophie and Tante Gaby began to talk about the call they must soon pay on their old friends next door. Of course, Grand-mère 'Toinette does not know that you are here. No one has dared to tell her. But my aunts are both dying to see their famous nephew and his daughter. And I too! Though, naturally, I have been forbidden to see you." Arcadie chuckled again.

"I told her you'd all come," Jessamyn said.

"You were right!" Arcadie held Lauré off at arm's length and studied her. "Such beautiful hair—like spun gold where the sun touches it. And you have the Beaudine eyes and Grand-mère's nose. You are not wholly *américaine*—the Creole is there too, despite the fair hair. I have been so eager to see you. New Orleans is full of cousins, but most are older and treat me as a child. The rest are mere babies. You are only one year older than I—you see, I have informed myself."

"I didn't even know I had a cousin in New Orleans," Lauré confessed. "My father never talks of his side of the family."

"I can well believe it." Arcadie nodded wisely. "My grandfather was furious when his youngest son became an actor instead of choosing the law, and of course Grand-mère has done always what Grand-père wished."

"But now that our grandfather is dead," Lauré said, "I should think—"

"Ah, but you don't know Grand-mère 'Toinette!" Arcadie broke in. "No one discusses with Grand-mère what she does not wish to discuss. The subject of Jules Beaudine is forbidden."

"Just the same I wish I could see her," Lauré said, a little wistfully.

Arcadie shook her head. "It could only be chance that would permit such a meeting. It is not possible otherwise. No matter—there will surely be ways for us to meet. Jessamyn's mother has invited me to her soirée day after tomorrow. I am looking forward to it." She paused a little breathlessly and then went on. "Is it true that you are an actress?"

Here it was again. "Oh, dear!" Lauré said. "You make it sound so wicked, somehow. I only wish it were true and that I were an actress. But I haven't been on the stage since I was younger than Jessamyn, and my father doesn't believe in my ambition to act, now that I'm grown."

"If Grand-mère knew you want to follow in your father's steps, she would be still more wild," Arcadie said. "It is surely best that you do not meet."

"Is our grandmother really such a frightening person?" Lauré asked.

"Frightening—yes. Because she will stand no nonsense at all. What she believes, she believes, and no one dares to cross her. Though she is not unkind—do not mistake me. I love her dearly. But if it were she visiting next door instead of Tante Sophie and Tante Gaby, I would not dare to be here now."

"Won't they tell her what you've done by coming over here?" Lauré asked.

"And confess their own curiosity? I think not." She turned with interest to Jessamyn. "Tell me, what do you hear of your brother Cole?"

"Nothing!" Jessamyn sighed. "He's just disappeared."

Arcadie shook her head sadly. "A foolish one—him. To throw away his life and so upset his family." Then she glanced with sudden interest over Lauré's shoulder. "This gentleman coming across the lawn—this is my Oncle Jules?"

Lauré turned and saw her father coming toward the summerhouse, very tall and straight and handsome. How proud she was of him, she thought, and how glad to present him to this newly found cousin.

Jules Beaudine took Arcadie's small hand and bent over it gallantly when Lauré introduced them. "So this is my little niece?" he said. "The child of my older brother. Your father died, my dear, some years after I left New Orleans. I never knew your mother."

"I was very young when they died in a yellow-fever epidemic," Arcadie said. "I do not remember them. I am happy to meet you, Oncle Jules."

She was more subdued now, a little awed and breathless in the presence of someone so famous.

Jessamyn, who had been watching the other house, plucked at Arcadie's sleeve. "They're looking for you," she whispered. "Both aunts are out on the front gallery and they are looking this way!"

Jules Beaudine had been standing well in the shadow, but now he glanced toward the house and moved at once into open sunlight. "My respected aunts!" he said, and strode across the lawn toward them.

"Ah, no!" Arcadie cried, and flew after him, but his strides were too long for her, and he reached the house before she did, while Jessamyn and Lauré trailed after them.

The two ladies in black stood in frozen dismay, clearly caught and not knowing which way to turn. Their nephew leaped up the steps and caught each in the strong embrace of an encircling arm.

"Sophronie!" he cried, "Gabrielle!" and kissed them soundly on their thin cheeks. Then he turned and beckoned to Lauré. "It is time you met your great-niece, my charming daughter. Lauré, these are your aunts Sophie and Gaby."

The two women said nothing at all. Only their eyes moved a little frantically, and their heads automatically made little nods of greeting as good manners required. Then they looked at each other and with one accord swept down the steps past their nephew and toward the carriage that waited at the curb. Arcadie made a gesture of despair.

"You see?" she whispered, and reluctantly followed them to the carriage.

Lauré felt indignant that his aunts should treat her father so and she half expected him to be angry. But he laughed out loud and made the carriage a deep bow as it pulled away from the curb.

"Fine!" he said. "Let them take an account of us home to my mother."

Jessamyn planted herself before him, eager as always to contribute something to the conversation. "They won't do that. Arcadie says her grandmother hasn't been told you're here. Everyone's afraid to tell her."

Jules Beaudine looked at the child with an air of displeasure which did not seem to awe her in the least. Then he said carelessly: "It doesn't matter. I have not come here to encumber myself with family problems."

Someone called to Jessamyn from the house and she ran off reluctantly. Lauré walked across the lawn with her father. He slipped her hand through the crook of his arm and smiled at her, all the sternness fading from his face.

"Thus far, how do you like New Orleans?" he asked.

"What I've seen is beautiful. And Mrs. Drummond is very kind. Do you know that she is giving a soirée for you day after tomorrow?"

He nodded. "I've been given to understand that you've not brought enough frocks for parties."

"I have no frocks for parties," she admitted. "Aunt Judith doesn't approve of frivolity."

Always his face was expressive, and she could sense his quick withdrawal from the subject—as if he wished to accept no responsibility for the life she had led with Aunt Judith, or to hear about its limitations, lest they reflect upon him. She was beginning to learn that he would enjoy her as a daughter as long as she was cheerful and did not trouble him in any way. But he was far from ready to accept the responsibilities of a father. And until he was, how could she ever persuade him to take her with him when he opened his company in the fall?

5. Ophelia or Kate?

SINCE Jessamyn ate her supper earlier, only the grownups were present that night.

Foster Drummond had returned from his trip in time for the evening meal, and Lauré met him for the first time. She found him a less impressive figure than Jules Beaudine. He was shorter and he lacked the actor's fine carriage. His stomach had turned into a small paunch from too much good eating, and he wore a heavy gold watch chain looped across it. Nevertheless, he was a man of considerable dignity, and one sensed his importance at a glance—an importance that was not self-importance, for undoubtedly he was a distinguished citizen in the business world of New Orleans.

He greeted his old friend Jules with pleasure and was cordial to Lauré, but he was more reserved than his Creole wife and he lacked her easy gaiety and exuberance. One sensed that he had troublesome matters on his mind, and while his son's name was not mentioned, Lauré suspected that worry over Cole must weigh him down considerably.

It was clear that the festivities of Carnival meant less to Foster Drummond than they did to his wife, and when she mentioned the ball they were to attend shortly before Mardi Gras, he sighed and looked at Lauré's father.

"I'm sure you'll enjoy this rigmarole a lot more than I will, Jules. The Creole in you probably thrives on Carnival, to say nothing of the actor. I go only because Celeste insists on it."

His wife echoed his sigh despairingly. "Foster could belong to more than one krewe if he wanted to. But everything is always business, business, business with him! I suppose I am fortunate that he's willing to go to these affairs at all."

"I go, my dear," Mr. Drummond said, not unkindly, "because I know you would perish if you were not a part of Carnival every year. Fortunately, the parades go down St. Charles, so we can view much of what goes on without discomfort. But I'm always glad for the peace of Lent."

"Do you expect your son home in time for Mardi Gras?" Jules Beaudine asked.

It was an innocent question, Lauré knew. Clearly no one had told him the details about Cole. Perhaps she should warn him, so that he would not blunder like this again.

Mr. and Mrs. Drummond exchanged pained looks, and Mrs. Drummond said, "At the moment we don't know exactly when he will be home."

The subject was quickly dropped, to Lauré's relief. She felt intensely sorry for poor Mrs. Drummond, who must somehow keep up appearances when her heart must be sick with anxiety over her son. How did Cole Drummond feel, she wondered, now that the results of his reckless actions had gone so far? What was he really like?

The next day she had an unexpected opportunity to learn something more about him. After church, a big Sunday dinner was served, and then everyone settled down for a lazy afternoon. Mrs. Drummond napped, while Mr. Drummond and Jules Beaudine went for a walk about the neighborhood, looking up old landmarks. Lauré retired to her own room to write a letter to her friend Maud in New York. It wasn't long, however, before Jessamyn appeared at her door.

"Will you come across the hall for a minute?" she asked. "I want to show you something."

Lauré followed the child to the door of a bedroom that was clearly Cole's. For a moment she was not sure that she should step into his private world without his leave. But after all, he was away and not using the room, and she found herself eager to discover more about so mysterious a young man.

There were no ruffles and frills about this room. The furniture looked comfortable and old—a narrow bed with a plain gray spread covering it, a scarred mahogany desk which must have served him through his school years, a bookcase well packed with books. Plainly they were books that were used and read and not there for mere show.

Lauré moved curiously toward the bookcase to discover some of the titles, but Jessamyn demanded her attention.

"Look!" the little girl cried. "This is what I wanted to show you. Cole made it all by himself when he was fourteen."

The object which held Jessamyn's interest was a handsome model of a Mississippi steamboat, paddle wheel and all, with a tiny wooden figure of the captain upon the bridge.

"You mustn't touch it," Jessamyn warned. "Cole lets me come in and look whenever I like—so long as I don't play with it."

"It's a very fine piece of work," Lauré said, studying the intricate details of the boat. It must have taken great patience to complete so perfect a duplication. What a contradictory sort of person Cole must be!

"And look over here," Jessamyn went on, gesturing toward the opposite wall.

Turning, Lauré saw that two crossed swords had been hung against the bare wall. They were odd-looking swords, with three grooved sides tapering to a vicious point.

"I don't suppose you've ever seen a real *colichemarde* before, have you?" Jessamyn asked. "Creole gentlemen used to duel with swords like that. Those very swords belonged to my grandfather on Mamma's side. She said he fought duels with them when he was young."

"Did Cole use a—?" Lauré began.

Jessamyn shook her head in scorn at such ignorance. "When the Americans came in they didn't know how to duel with swords, so everyone had to change to pistols. That's what Cole fought with, of course—a dueling pistol. Papa says pistols are really lots more deadly than the sword, but I would have liked to see a sword duel. It sounds more exciting."

Lauré, thinking of Cole, who had nearly killed a man with a pistol, shivered and turned again to the bookcase.

"Someday," said Jessamyn, "I'm going to read all those books, just like Cole does."

Lauré let a hand stray along the titles of the Waverley Novels by Sir Walter Scott. Somehow she always loved the feel of books. There were volumes of poetry too, by Tennyson and Lord Byron. She had read a good deal of Tennyson, but Aunt Judith would never allow anything written by Byron under her roof. Next came some books by Washington Irving, and some by the modern writer Mark Twain. There was a shelf of old schoolbooks too, and a shelf of Greek philosophers. Because of the books, Lauré had an increasing wish to like Cole Drummond and to find excuses for him.

She turned to Jessamyn thoughtfully. "This—this gambling—has he done very much of it?"

"Who?" Jessamyn asked.

"Your brother. You said he'd lost money that he was in debt for."

"It's not the gambling that matters so much," Jessamyn said. "Papa says all Creoles love to gamble. My father could pay Cole's debts if he wanted to. The main trouble is that Cole doesn't want to work in Papa's bank and learn to be a vice-president or something. That's what started all this trouble." She yawned and looked at Lauré as if for inspiration. "What shall we do now?"

Lauré had just spied a volume of Shakespeare's plays in the bookcase and she drew it out eagerly. Perhaps she would come back and borrow Byron later, but for now, this was what she wanted.

"I'm going to find a quiet spot and read for a while," she told Jessamyn.

The little girl looked disappointed, but decided to play with the children next door. When she had gone, the house was pleasantly quiet, and Lauré went through the cool upper hall and down the lovely staircase, her hand resting lightly on the rail. What a perfect staircase for an actress making an entrance, she thought. An actress in a beautiful silken gown that rippled about her toes, just showing the point of a satin slipper as she descended, and rustling in a train behind her. Lauré went down step by graceful step, pretending. Of course there should be admiring young men at the foot of the stairs watching her.

She practiced all the way to the lower floor, faltering in her balance only once, around the turn where the steps turned into wedges. There was a library downstairs—she had glimpsed it yesterday—and there she might find a quiet haven where she could read and dream.

The library door stood open, and she went in softly, closing it behind her. What a huge room it was—cool and dim and shuttered. If she wanted to read, she would need more light, and she chose sunlight, flinging open one tall shutter so that a sunny shaft cut through the shadows and fell upon a long leather couch backed against the fireplace. The room was handsomely furnished, with a carved library table and several easy chairs. And of course there were bookcases all along one wall. Set after leather-bound set occupied the shelves, but they did not look as well worn from reading as did the books in Cole's room upstairs.

At one end of the couch were several cushions, and Lauré

plumped them up and lay back against them, relaxed and at ease.

Perhaps she made herself a little too comfortable, or perhaps the huge dinner she had eaten so hungrily had made her drowsy, for her attention would not focus for long on *Julius Caesar.* Although there was no really important woman's part in the play, it was still one of her favorites. She could usually visualize her father as Brutus, and the words would come to life and stir her as they had as a child when she had seen him play the role.

But not today. Not even when she tried reading Brutus' words aloud. Before long the book settled comfortably on her chest, her lashes flickered on her cheeks, she took a long deep breath—and was asleep. The February sun moved along its arc and the shadows in the library shifted their pattern.

At the first the voice seemed a part of Lauré's dreams, speaking to her softly from a faraway place. "Can this be the Lady of Shalott?" it said.

What strange words were spoken in dreams, she mused, still half asleep. Then someone seemed to bend over her, and the voice broke the spell by chuckling.

"No—this lady's not bound for Camelot. That's no sheaf of lilies in her hands, but a book. Shakespeare, I do believe. A girl in New Orleans who reads Shakespeare!"

She opened her eyes and sat up quickly. Her gaze traveled up the line of gray trousers to a neat waistcoat and widening shoulders. Then at last to the dark, rather brooding face above, its somber lines livened by gray eyes that regarded her with interest and amusement.

"I don't know where you came from, or who you are," he

said. "But please don't go away. I'd have returned home sooner if I'd known the family had a guest like you."

"Then you—you must be Cole Drummond?" she faltered.

"Sh-sh!" He waggled a quieting finger at her. "Don't announce me to the world. There'll be a hullabaloo as soon as they find I'm here. Let's postpone the commotion for a while and talk about you. Since you're not the Lady of Shalott, what is your name?"

"Lauré," she told him. "My father and I are visiting your parents."

His eyebrows were as dark as his thick dark hair, and they made crescents of astonishment above gray, mirth-filled eyes.

"A French name?" he said. "With all that fair hair?"

"I'm half Creole," she admitted, feeling somehow mesmerized, so that she could not get her feet down upon the everyday earth.

"Better and better," he said. "I too, *Mam'selle*"—he made an exaggerated little bow—"am half Creole. But this is a dangerous mingling, as you may have discovered. There's a piece of me that wants to go one way, a part that pulls another. Between the two I don't always know who or what I am."

"I feel that way too," Lauré said earnestly. "Sometimes I'm sure I want only—" and then unhappy memory swept back upon her and her expression turned to one of dismay. "Is—is it safe for you to be here? Are they looking for you?"

"They'll look quickly enough when they have an inkling that I'm here," he told her. "But I don't think a soul saw me

65

come in and—"

"No," she said. "I don't mean that. I mean is it possible that the police—that man in the hospital—the duel—?"

This time he looked completely mystified. "Perhaps you're still dreaming. Sometimes that happens to me, so that when I'm waking up I mix the real with the dream for a while."

"No, no, no!" she cried, a little frantic now. "That man you—you wounded in a duel— If he dies—"

Cole took both her hands into his to calm her. "*I* fought a duel? *I* wounded someone? What on earth are you talking about?"

"Didn't you gamble away money that didn't belong to you?" she demanded.

"Gamble? I've never gone in for that sort of thing."

"But Jessamyn said—"

He whooped in sudden delight. "Jessamyn! Of course— I might have guessed. Jessamyn plans to be New Orlean's greatest novelist and she is always practicing. Her head is filled with romances about dueling, gambling, and all the rest of New Orleans' history. I'm afraid she has taken you in rather thoroughly."

Lauré was quite still for a moment. After all the tender-hearted concern she had spent on him, after the way she had practically sided against society to excuse him—and now—!

He sat down on the couch beside her. "I'm sorry," he said. "I'm sure Jessamyn did a fine job of making me a fasci-nating scoundrel. If it will comfort you any, I *am* the family's black sheep just now. My mother feels that I'm about to break her heart, and I wouldn't be surprised if my father turned me out entirely."

He spoke lightly, but there was an undercurrent of the serious beneath his words, as if he was not altogether joking.

"I suppose that's what made me believe Jessamyn," Lauré said, feeling decidedly foolish. "I've heard hints of your misdeeds, though no one says exactly what they are. What do they mean?"

He yawned, the back of a hand over his mouth. "Forgive me—I've had a long trip. Let's not go into my offenses right now. Just think how much more interesting I'll be if you don't know the truth about me." The gray eyes twinkled at her, though his firm, strong mouth did not smile.

She edged away from him, not knowing what to say or do. Cole Drummond seemed a thoroughly puzzling person. He did not fit the pattern of any young man she had ever known—in a book or out. Even if he hadn't fought a duel or indulged in wicked escapades, he still made her curious.

He reached over and touched the volume of plays she held. "Since you read Shakespeare, tell me your favorite heroine."

Now he was walking right into her private dreams and ambitions, and she was not sure she wanted to give him an answer.

"Whom do you think I should choose?" she countered.

For a man, his dark lashes were very long and thick, but there was nothing feminine about him. He studied her appraisingly.

"Let me see—what role would be best loved by the Lady of Shalott? Ophelia, perhaps? Yes, that's it, of course—Hamlet's Ophelia."

Now she was annoyed with him. Never, never had she cared for the part of poor, gentle, mad Ophelia.

"You're not a very good judge," she said. "If I were an actress—" she hesitated just an instant, "I'd choose the role of Katharine in *The Taming of the Shrew.*"

He laughed out loud in delight. "No—never! Not Kate for you. You would never fit the role."

Her exasperation was growing. So that was the way she appeared to him—someone meek and mild, the very opposite of Kate.

He saw her indignation and stopped laughing. "Don't mind," he said. "I suppose we all like to pick parts in our reading that are the opposite of those we play in real life."

He had gone too far. She forgot her uncertainty and jumped to her feet. It seemed suddenly necessary to show him how wrong he was in linking her with Ophelia. Across the room she stalked and back again, dramatically, and spoke Kate's words upon her meeting with Petruchio: " 'They call me Katharine that do talk of me.' "

And while he watched in proper astonishment, she played a bit of the scene for him, showing him Kate with her words, her every move and gesture. He was all attention now. She saw no mockery in his face, and her knowledge of an arrested audience went giddily to her head so that she really launched herself into the scene.

It was then Mrs. Drummond walked into the room. "I thought I heard voices," she said, while Lauré halted in confusion. She saw her son and flew across the room, her arms out. Cole rose from the couch and embraced her.

"When did you get home, Cole?" she cried. "Why didn't you come to see me at once?"

"I knew you'd be napping, Mother," he said. "And when I came in here I found your guest. Do you know that you have a find for your next theatricals? She can play Kate in *The Taming of the Shrew* as if she'd been born to the stage!"

Mrs. Drummond threw an amused look at Lauré. "But of course she can. Why not—when she *was* born to the stage? Cole, this is Lauré Beaudine, Jules Beaudine's daughter. You know—the famous actor."

Cole's eyes were upon Lauré over his mother's shoulder, and she found herself blushing guiltily, which was foolish, of course. There had been no reason to tell him who she was.

"I see," he said and sounded oddly sober. "No wonder she plays the part so well."

His mother was concerned at the moment only with her son. "Come upstairs and talk to me, Cole. I'm so happy that you're home. Now you'll be here for the soirée tomorrow night, and for the Carnival ball. Nothing could be more perfect. Especially if you've given up this other nonsense. You'll excuse us, Lauré?"

Lauré nodded. Cole made her a somewhat formal bow and followed his mother out of the room. When they'd gone, Lauré sat down on the couch again, feeling keyed up and not at all ready to be quiet. The words "plays the part so well" echoed in her ears, yet she was not wholly elated. All in all, she had found this encounter with Cole Drummond a disturbing one—one to make her more angry than pleased.

As she sat there thinking about what had happened, words her father had spoken returned to her. That ridiculous thing he had said about falling in love with the first young man she met—and the possibility that it might be Cole Drummond. She could tell him something about that now. She had met Cole Drummond and she had found him on the whole a rather dismaying young man. She was not even sure that she liked him.

Having settled that matter to her satisfaction, she went upstairs to her room, smiling faintly and not at all aware that she smiled.

6. *Creole Soirée*

In February the evenings could still be pleasantly cool in New Orleans. A little breeze blew in Lauré's open window as she dressed for Mrs. Drummond's soirée. She felt both excited and a little frightened over the coming party. Never in her life had she been to an affair of this sort, and she was fearful of doing the wrong thing, of appearing ignorant and clumsy—particularly before her father.

More than anything else she was doubtful of her dress. She stood before the wide mirror over her dresser and tried to see herself from all angles, to see herself with strange eyes looking at a girl she had never beheld before. If the guests thought her dowdy, she would do her father no honor. And if he looked at her ashamed, she would want to crawl away and die.

The dress was white lawn, drawn in at the waist, smooth in front, with a gathered fullness at the back. It was utterly plain except for a deep inset of lace in the upper bodice, dressing it up to some extent. She had no idea what other women would be wearing, but to her eyes the girl in the mirror looked hopelessly plain and unfashionable.

There was a tap at the door. Lauré hesitated a moment before she said, "Come in."

It was Mrs. Drummond, with an eager Jessamyn at her side. Jessamyn was not being permitted to remain up for the party tonight, but she meant to stay as close as possible to all the preparations. And she was quite unabashed in Lauré's presence. Yesterday Lauré had confronted the child with her monstrous story about Cole. But Jessamyn had only laughed delightedly.

"You believed me!" she cried. "Cole says that's what an author has to do—make people believe in the stories he tells. So now I'm writing it into a book. Maybe I'll let you read it sometimes."

Lauré had tried to explain the difference between putting a make-believe story into a book and presenting one as gospel truth about real people, but she was not sure she had made much impression.

Now Jessamyn circled her critically, while Mrs. Drummond plainly made an effort to be kind.

"You look very sweet and girlish," she said. "Turn around, Lauré, please, so I can see how it looks at the back."

Lauré turned, and Mrs. Drummond patted and pulled, her doubtful expression quite visible to Lauré in the mirror. As she had expected, the dress was wrong.

"It doesn't look much like a party dress," said Jessamyn, pursing up her mouth the way Miss Willis the dressmaker did.

"Hush, dear," her mother said gently. "Tonight will be very informal, with mostly relatives coming. You know, Lauré, in New Orleans practically everyone is related in some way to everyone else. So we can afford to be tolerant—we belong to one another."

None of this sounded reassuring, and Lauré's already fading courage went down another notch. Perhaps she ought to develop some serious ailment at the last minute, find some excuse not to attend.

Celeste Drummond looked charming in a frock of pale-rose satin with a *décolletage* which set off to good effect her plump, smooth neck and shoulders. Beside her in the mirror Lauré knew she looked about thirteen and both awkward and plain.

Arcadie had said she would be coming tonight, and the pretty Arcadie would of course be correctly and charmingly gowned. Lauré was sure her little cousin would never be unkind, but perhaps she would be pitying toward a girl from the North who didn't know what to wear for a New Orleans soirée.

There was nothing to be said, however, and no one suggested that anything could be done. When Mrs. Drummond and Jessamyn left, Lauré faced herself again in the mirror. Should she go to her father and ask his advice? He was a man of the world—he would know what was best for her to do. If it proved that she might disgrace him, perhaps he would aid her in a story of sudden illness.

She went quickly to the door and then paused with her hand on the knob. Jules Beaudine was not one who liked other people's troubles brought to him, as his daughter had quickly discovered. He might himself at times be thrust into depths of depression, black moods, when everyone about him tiptoed with care. He'd had one of these on the train coming down here. But he wanted smiles and good cheer from his daughter, and she suspected that he had very little notion about what might be going on inside her heart and head. This fact left her with a lonely ache she could not put into words. Nevertheless, he *was* her father, and perhaps it was time for him to accept the responsibility and realize that she had problems too.

She pulled open her door and went briskly down the hall to his room. "It's Lauré," she called in answer to his question.

He came to let her in, and she stepped uncertainly into the room. He was wearing well-fitting black trousers of fine broadcloth and a white waistcoat. The linen of his shirt gleamed fresh and brightly white beneath black suspenders.

"Ready for the party?" he asked, as he picked up two silver-backed military brushes and began to brush his thick dark hair back from his forehead, watching himself in a mirror.

She stood just behind him, drooping a little, peering around him at her own dejected image. Cole Drummond would never see her as the Lady of Shalott tonight. Even Ophelia could do better than this.

"My dress," she said, "—it's all wrong. Dowdy. Without any style. Even Jessamyn knew I looked awful, though her mother tried to be polite and kind."

With a last smoothing of his dark hair, he set the brushes down and turned to look at her. "I thought you were getting some new frocks. I asked Celeste to take care of whatever you needed and let me have the bill."

"There's been no time," Lauré said miserably. "This party came up too soon."

"M-m," he said, "I see. Turn around and walk across the room."

She did as he told her, horribly self-conscious. She could feel the dress bunch around her waist and pull tight at the shoulders as she moved.

"You look," he said smiling a little, "like an immigrant maid just arrived from the old country and trying to mimic our ways, instead of being herself."

She felt tears sting her eyes at his words, and she blinked them back angrily. Her head came up and she returned his look with something less than her usual admiration for him. She had come to him for help, and he had in effect slapped her across the face.

"That's better," he said. "A little spirit always helps." And then he surprised her by putting his hand under her chin and tilting it, bending to kiss her on the cheek.

"Lauré, Lauré!" he said. "You tell me you want to be an actress. Then be one! An actress can play any role she must with what she has. Don't you know that it's not the gown that makes a woman beautiful? It's the woman who makes a gown beautiful."

She listened in astonishment, not sure of what he meant. He went on with that sparking of magnetism that always swept his listeners along. "Haven't you seen lovely dresses on women who looked dowdy in them? And haven't you seen a beautiful woman make a hopeless dress seem the height of fashion?"

"But—but I'm not beautiful," she said.

He tapped his knuckles beneath her chin in reproach. "If you are a good enough actress you can give the effect of beauty."

She wanted more of this reassurance desperately. "But Aunt Judith said—"

"Your Aunt Judith is not here. I am. And I am a man who has seen a good many beautiful women. As a child you had a funny, intriguing little face that always appealed to me. I could sense what you would grow into. That growing has long since begun, though you haven't noticed it. Do you still believe in charms, Lauré—as you used to when you were a little girl?"

"I—I don't know," she said, at a loss as to his meaning. He crossed the room to a table where a vase of white roses stood. When he turned back to her he held one white rose in his hand.

"A talisman for beauty," he said. "Wear this tonight and you'll be more beautiful than the women with jewels."

She took the rose from him wonderingly and held it up to the lace at the front of her dress.

He shook his head. "No—not there. Here." He tucked the rose into her hair near one temple. "Perfect! Now straighten your shoulders and look in the mirror. No girl who droops can ever be beautiful."

She raised her shoulders and lifted her chin, smiling a little as she stepped toward the mirror. It was true. The girl in the glass looked different. Not really beautiful, perhaps, but no longer like an immigrant maid.

Her father nodded approvingly. "Now you are the daughter of Jules Beaudine. You are enough in yourself—you don't need frivolous adornment, much as it would satisfy your feminine heart. Tonight I shall be proud of you."

Love for her father choked her. She wished she dared fling her arms about his neck and kiss him soundly, but he had never liked demonstrative gestures from her. It was as though he saved all tempestuous emotions for the stage.

"Thank you, Father," she said softly, and turned toward the door.

As she went he sent the verse of a Shakespeare sonnet ringing after her.

> " 'The rose looks fair, but fairer we it deem
> For that sweet odour which doth in it live.' "

She smiled at him and flew back to her room, knowing what he meant. He had given her more than a rose tonight; he had given her that beauty within, which would truly make her fair.

She waited quietly in her room, careful not to crush her dress or disturb the sweetly scented rose, until Jessamyn came to whisper that she was to go downstairs. Gracefully Lauré walked past her into the hall, remembering the walk she had practiced endlessly at home in New York—a walk that made her seem to drift effortlessly and with a proud carriage. Jessamyn was her first test.

The child watched her, puzzled. "That rose looks nice in your hair," she said. "You—you look different."

"I *am* different!" Lauré told her, and started downstairs.

Her father waited for her on the lovely, curving staircase, and she went down on his arm, feeling as though she floated. Once, on the way, he pressed her hand, and she knew everything was all right and that tonight she would really prove to him what an actress she was.

A certain fillip might have been added if Cole Drummond could have been standing in the hallway at the foot of the stairs, but he was nowhere in sight. She was not even sure he would attend the party, in spite of his mother's wishes.

He had scarcely been in view since he had come upon her in the library yesterday. She had seen him at the table last night, but he had been quiet, saying nothing about his trip away from New Orleans, and afterward he had disappeared until supper again tonight.

Having decided that she did not particularly like him, she had been prepared to be a little remote and cool toward him when next she saw him. It was disappointing that she had been given no opportunity to put him in his place. He had scarcely seemed to see her at meals, and was busy with his own affairs otherwise. The disapproval of his parents had been clearly apparent, though they were being polite in front of guests. Cole, however, seemed to notice them no more than he noticed her. It was as if all his thoughts and being were turned upon some faraway matter and he was hardly aware of those in his immediate vicinity. Not even the great Jules Beaudine had distracted him for long, though Lauré had been gratified to see that he woke up long enough to pay attention when he was introduced to the actor, and that he listened rather intently when Jules Beaudine was speaking.

Now as she and her father went downstairs, Lauré saw that guests had begun to arrive and she was glad to face them at her father's side. His air of proud regard for her was a reminder and a help.

The men and women were separating into different groups, she saw, with the ladies chattering of household topics or the latest gossip, while the gentlemen discussed business matters, sports, and other masculine subjects. Lauré was happy when her father did not bow to this division, but kept her at his side and let members of both groups come to them.

As the guests were presented, one after another, many of them identified as remote relatives, Lauré's confidence began to grow. These people seemed to find her attractive, and perhaps some of her father's greatness rubbed off on her a little, as long as she stood by his side. Always she looked for Arcadie, but nowhere did she see the gay little face of her cousin.

Not everyone in the gathering was well dressed. Creoles had no hesitation about showing individuality and independence when it came to clothes. One sensed a frugality that might keep a war-impoverished lady wearing a frock long after it was out of style. There was more than one exaggerated bustle in evidence, in a day when the bustle had faded to a mere fullness at the back.

At a New Orleans party there was a good deal of music and dancing—both beloved of the Orleanian. There were always those who were ready to sing and play, and the guests applauded the talented among themselves with loving warmth. The first waltz Lauré danced with her father, and she knew she would always remember it.

The great handsome room was alive with lights in crystal chandeliers—electric lights in this section of the city. It was a double room, really, opened into one, vast in its proportions, with high ceilings, two fireplaces, and carved marble mantels. Enormous full-length mirrors graced either end of the room, reflecting the brilliance of chandeliers, setting the jewels of the women twinkling. The high ceilings made room for echoing laughter and the lilting sound of the music.

Whirling in her father's arms, Lauré had a strange sense

of unreality. Was she really here in the Garden District of New Orleans? Would all this suddenly fade like Cinderella's vanishing coach and leave her dreaming wistfully in Aunt Judith's dark parlor? Could this be Lauré Beaudine dancing at such a fine party in the arms of a man who was famous everywhere in the country? a man who regarded her with tender pride because she was his daughter? Oh, how easy it was to be lovely if only one were loved! Tonight was almost like being a little girl again—only nicer.

The dance came to an end, and suddenly a young man was bowing before her, asking to be presented. Mrs. Drummond introduced him as Marcel Duval, and before Lauré had quite recovered from the impact of his admiring gaze, she was being carried away in a breathless schottische. Thank goodness for the dancing lessons her father had insisted upon when she was small, in spite of Aunt Judith!

Conversation was hardly possible, but she could glimpse his handsome face as they moved together. A Creole face, surely—she was beginning to recognize the stamp. Cole had the dark hair of the Creole, but his eyes were gray, his chin firm-jawed and American, his mouth straight. This young man had a gentler mouth, full-lipped like that of Jules Beaudine, and his eyes were warm and ardent.

"I've been longing to meet you," he whispered when there was a break in the dancing and they paused to catch their breaths. "Arcadie, your cousin, told me about you—a blond ice maiden from the North, yet with Creole blood in her veins. What a combination!"

No one had ever made Lauré such a speech before, and she felt breathless again and at a loss.

"I—I thought Arcadie was to be here tonight?" she faltered.

He drew her skillfully through the throng of guests toward a French door, and before she knew what he was about, they were outside on the wide gallery. Light from the room behind fell through doors and windows, and a half-moon gilded the shadows in the garden. She was not sure it was proper to be here alone with this young man, but she didn't particularly want to help herself.

"This is better—yes?" he said. "Now we can talk a little before we return to the dancing. In there someone would steal you from me at once." He reached for her hand and held it lightly. "For safety," he said, "so that you will not run away."

She had no skill at this sort of thing and it made her uncomfortable. Again she tried the subject of Arcadie.

"Do you know my cousin well?" she asked.

"Indeed, yes," he assured her. "The Duvals occupy the next house to Madame 'Toinette Beaudine on the Rue Royale. Arcadie hoped to come tonight, but—bad fortune!—someone reported to her grand-mère that Jules Beaudine had come to New Orleans and was being entertained by the Drummonds. So she would not permit 'Cadie to come. Thus I am your cousin's emissary. But now that I have seen you—far more."

To her dismay, Lauré felt a sudden desire to giggle. Young Marcel Duval didn't know her at all, nor she him. She could almost hear Aunt Judith's voice commenting tartly that it was foolish to make flowery speeches on such slight acquaintance. Yet he was not, somehow, ridiculous. The romantic air suited him well, and he seemed born to it. I was not necessary for her to believe in his words.

"Are you attending any of the Carnival balls, Mam'selle Lauré?" he asked, and she could only shake her head.

He started to speak again, when a shadow across the lawn detached itself abruptly from the summerhouse and came toward them. It was Cole Drummond, and Marcel held out his hand at sight of him.

"My good friend Cole! So you are back from the bayous? And how does it go—this incomprehensible project of yours?"

Cole shrugged as he took Marcel's hand. "*Comme ci, comme ça,* as you'd say." He turned to Lauré. "My dance," he said calmly. "Forgive us, Marcel." And before Lauré could so much as protest or assent, she had been whirled back into the lighted room and into another waltz.

She was not at all sure that she liked what had happened, but she had a feeling that it wouldn't make much difference to Cole if she told him so. Perhaps she could pique him by speaking of Marcel.

"Who is that very attractive young man?" she asked.

"Marcel Duval is the son of your Grandmother 'Toinette's lawyer. And I might as well warn you, that he makes pretty speeches to girls at the flick of an eyelash, the way all Creoles do. I suppose I'm jealous of his ability and that's why I snatched you back inside."

"So you were eavesdropping?" Lauré said.

"Why not? You invaded my territory and started talking for all the garden to hear."

"Why weren't you inside at your mother's party?" Lauré asked heatedly. "I know she was looking for you."

"I *am* here," he said, and suddenly he smiled at her. "You

don't seem to be managing the Kate role very well tonight—not with a white rose in your hair. You look much more like Juliet."

She said nothing at all, her irritation with him increasing.

"A man named John Boyle O'Reilly wrote a poem called 'A White Rose,'" he said in her ear as they followed the waltzing circle about the room. "The words suit you. Let's see—how do they go?

> " 'O, the red rose is a falcon,
> And the white rose is a dove.' "

She knew he was teasing her, but she wished the white rose out of her hair. In spite of her playing Kate for him, he still identified her with Ophelia. But before she could object further, he had waltzed her back to her father's side, and left her there, looking a little amused as he went, like a proper son, to make apologies to his mother.

Lauré felt like stamping her foot, and then realized that her father was watching her.

"So you've made a conquest already?" he said.

She glanced at him, startled, thinking he meant Cole, but he had turned his head to look across the room at Marcel Duval, who had come in and was dancing with another girl.

"I saw him waltz you outside. A girl might lose her heart, and her head with it, to that one. Very sensible of Cole to bring you inside. Do you remember our talk in New York? I hope you're being sensible."

She smiled at him confidently. "I remember. But so far you're wrong, Father. So far I've met two young men and I've fallen in love with neither one."

"That's my girl," he said. "Flirt all you like. But stay away from love. It leads only to torment and tears. When you're older perhaps—a suitable marriage. But I want you to have some fun first."

How strange he was! He talked to her as no other adult ever had, and she was not always sure that his advice was sound. A "suitable marriage"—what a cold ring that had! Her mother had not made a suitable marriage and perhaps she had died because of the fact, yet she had been beloved and happy.

There was no time for long thoughts at such a party, however, and she quickly forgot them, dancing the hours away with other partners, listening to other compliments—all a heady, delightful mixture. Cole did not come to dance with her again, but Marcel continued to hover near, and when elaborate refreshments were served after midnight, he made himself her partner. Jules Beaudine had been firmly annexed by a handsome lady of middle age who seemed to amuse him.

It was nearly two o'clock when at last the party was over and she went up to bed, her feet burning and her head awhirl. But once she lay on her pillow, her eyelids drooping, she could think triumphantly of the evening. She was going to be a success in New Orleans. She had quickly forgotten that she was supposed to be acting a part and had enjoyed herself naturally without fear of criticism or disapproval. All that was asked of her was that she be gay and young. This was a town she could learn to love.

Strangely, however, it was the Lady of Shalott she thought of before she fell asleep. What was the story? The Lady had sat weaving in her tower, held there by a spell. If she looked down toward Camelot, a curse would fall upon her. Then into the vista of her mirror a knight had come riding.

> "His broad clear brow in sunlight glowed;
> On burnished hooves his war horse trode;
> From underneath his helmet flowed
> His coal-black curls as on he rode,
>   As he rode down to Camelot.
> From the bank and from the river
> He flashed into the crystal mirror,
> 'Tirra lirra,' by the river
>   Sang Sir Lancelot.
>
> "She left the web, she left the loom,
> She made three paces through the room,
> She saw the water lily bloom,
> She saw the helmet and the plume,
>   She looked down to Camelot.
> Out flew the web and floated wide;
> The mirror cracked from side to side:
> 'The curse is come upon me,' cried
>   The Lady of Shalott."

Lauré smiled sleepily, remembering the verses. The Lady of the poem had given in to her fate rather easily. Lauré Beaudine would never be like that, even if Sir Lancelot should come riding.

She slept soundly, luxuriously, late into the morning, with no Aunt Judith to call her a lie-abed.

7. Meeting in the French Market

TODAY," Mrs. Drummond announced at breakfast several days after the party, "Lauré must see something of the old New Orleans. It is a disgrace that she has been in town for more than a week and has not so much as seen the Vieux Carré—the French Quarter."

Foster Drummond had left earlier for his bank, and for once Cole was at the table too, as well as Jessamyn, Lauré, and her father.

Lauré waited expectantly, ready to go anywhere. Jessamyn promptly asked if she might stay home and go too, and was told that she must of course attend school as usual. Neither Cole nor Jules Beaudine said anything.

"I'm going to drive to the French Market this morning," Mrs. Drummond went on, "so this is a good opportunity. Would you like to go, Jules?"

The actor shook his head. "Thanks, but I think not." He spoke a little stiffly, and Lauré wondered how much hurt might lie behind his avoidance of that section of the city where he had lived as a boy.

Mrs. Drummond nodded sympathetically. "Then, Cole, you must come with us—as company for Lauré."

"And to carry your basket, Mother?" he asked, teasing.

"I shall take Marie for basket-carrying—you can be free to entertain Lauré and show her the sights."

There was a little silence, and Lauré did not look at Cole. She was sure he would get out of the request somehow. He had paid no attention to her since the soirée, and she suspected that most of the time he forgot about her existence.

To her surprise, however, he agreed. "All right, I'll play guide for Lauré if you'd like me to," he said, and so it was arranged.

After breakfast, when the victoria was ready, they got into the carriage and started off. Cole sat beside Lauré, while Marie, the maid, sat on a drop seat opposite.

Down broad St. Charles Avenue they rolled, past white-columned homes and green lawns, around the circle where the statue of Robert E. Lee, atop a tall, slim column, faced forever north—because of course he would never turn his back on a Yankee, as every Orleanian was quick to inform you.

As they crossed Canal Street, Lauré had a glimpse of that wide business vista, and then the carriage, picking its way more slowly now among mule-drawn drays and other vehicles, moved into another world. Cole seemed to wake up and look about him with more interest.

"This is where old New Orleans began," he said. "The Vieux Carré—the Old Square."

Now the streets were narrow and shadowy, the little houses rising flush with the banquettes—as sidewalks were called—their upper galleries often protruding over the walk to form a shelter from sun and rain. There was no space between one house and the next, yet each had its individual character and façade, being painted a soft peach, or pale green, or faded rose.

The houses were no more than two or three stories high, and along the face of each ran the famous galleries that were an intricate lacework of cast iron. In the early days, Cole said, hand-wrought iron, made by the slaves, had been used, but little of that remained, and these balconies were also old and equally beautiful.

Behind the galleries rose tall green jalousies, shuttered doors, closed against the sun, so that every house looked as though it slept.

"This is Royal Street," Mrs. Drummond said, and Lauré felt a quickening of attention.

This was the street where she had been born, not far from the Beaudine house. On this street stood the home of her Creole family.

"Will you tell me, please, if we pass the Beaudine house?" she asked, suddenly alert and eager.

"Watch for it, Cole," his mother said. "You see things more quickly than I. We are going past it because your father wished you to see it, Lauré. He spoke to me of this just before we left."

It had never seemed to Lauré that she had ever had any roots. She had lived most of her life in her aunt's house in New York, but she had no feeling of having a "home" as other girls meant the word. "Home" to her meant only the life of the stage and all the enfolding love she had known in those gypsy days of one-night stands before her mother died and her father became famous. New Orleans had seemed little more than a name to her—a city she had never expected to see. Yet now, before her very eyes, was unfolding the place where her forebears had lived, where her father had grown up and her grandmother still resided in the house of the Beaudines.

Cole touched her arm lightly. "There it is—across the street. The house with the arched carriageway."

The victoria slowed at a word from Mrs. Drummond, while the driver of a dray shouted impatiently from behind.

They paid no attention, but moved slowly past the narrow little house, weathered by sun and rain to a soft cream. Upstairs, in the iron of the gallery's leaf design, was set an elaborately scrolled "B" for Beaudine, and Lauré, seeing it there, had a sense of age and history.

As they passed the carriage entrance, she peered through an arched tunnel that opened in the rear upon a sunny courtyard. She had a glimpse of banana plants and bamboo, and of a small fountain where water played. Then the picture was gone and the carriage had turned off Royal Street toward the river.

For a moment Lauré was afraid tears would come. She looked ahead and blinked her lashes fast, choking back the lump in her throat. So small a glimpse it had been—nothing at all, really. And yet she had felt a pull of emotion she would never have believed possible. She had a queer longing to cry out to the coachman to stop the carriage so that she might jump out and run back to that house, hurry through the arched tunnel to the courtyard, and stand there in sun and shade, feeling that she had truly come "home."

Cole began to talk softly in the manner of a not-too-intrusive guide. "Riding along the streets like this, we see only the backs of the houses," he told her. "They live their real lives facing the inner courtyards. Mother must take you to visit a Creole family so that you can see what the houses are like inside."

She swallowed the lump and stole a grateful look at him. He was watching her kindly, as if he understood the emotion that had so unexpectedly shaken her.

"The sad thing," he went on, "is the way everything is crumbling to ruin. Look at that wall—the bricks have broken from one corner. Over there someone has made ugly patches without bothering to paint them over. And the iron is rusting through on that gallery across the street."

Slowly she was able to thrust back the emotion that had shaken her and look about with a more objective air. It was true that marks of decay were visible everywhere—here a crooked chimney, there a roof where slate was missing.

"What a shame!" she cried. "How can people neglect a place like this? This section must be different from any other city in America."

"Riffraff began to move in after the war between North and South," Mrs. Drummond said. "The Creoles were poverty-stricken, and many of them sold their houses and moved away. Some who still had money began to seek larger houses elsewhere."

"But my grandmother has stayed," Lauré said, and found that she sounded almost proud.

"There are few like your Grand-mère 'Toinette," Mrs. Drummond agreed, smiling. "She is one of those fighting for the life of the Vieux Carré. Not a month ago she—who seldom steps across Canal Street—came to my husband's bank and bullied him into a contribution larger than he intended to make, all for the sake of her committee and its purpose."

"I wouldn't like to be the one to oppose her," Cole said, a note of admiration in his voice. "She's not one of your Cre-oles who closes her doors and pretends that the rest of the world doesn't exist. She may not altogether approve of the world, but she isn't going to let it take the Vieux Carré away from her. The last time I saw her she was in a dudgeon over what was happening in the old Pontalba Buildings. 'Pigs in the Pontalba!' she was crying, and thumping that gold-headed cane of hers on the floor as if she were chasing the very pigs with it."

"Yet she didn't grow up here," Mrs. Drummond put in. "Her family branch of the Fortiers never belonged to the Vieux Carré the way the Beaudines did. Your grandmother, Lauré, grew up in one of the beautiful plantation houses across the river."

Cole said, "Look—here's Jackson Square, with the Pontalba Buildings along either side."

Lauré had seen pictures of this square in a book. There was an expanse of park, with a statue of General Jackson at the center and a tall iron fence all around. The carriage turned past the graceful cathedral, with the Cabildo, once the house of state, and the Presbytery, the house of the church, on either side of it. Then it turned again past the handsome Spanish buildings that the Baroness de Pontalba had built as the first apartment buildings in America.

"Stop a moment!" Cole said to the coachman. "You go ahead in the carriage, Mother, but let me take Lauré through the square on foot. I want her to meet the general. We'll see you at the market."

His mother agreed, and Cole jumped out, holding out his hand to Lauré. She stepped down eagerly, glad of the chance to stretch her legs and see more of this famous square.

Cole led the way to an iron gate at one side, and they went through and onto the ordered walks of the park. There was tropical foliage all about—plants and trees that Lauré had never seen before—but her interest focused on the great bronze statue, greenish now and streaked with the soot of years. Jackson rode a prancing horse, balanced unbeliev-ably on its slender hind legs, his cocked hat raised in salute as he rode past the Cathedral of St. Louis.

"This used to be the Place d'Armes in the old days," Cole said. "A good deal of New Orleans history has been written here."

She glanced at him wonderingly. His eyes were alight with interest, instead of absent-minded or amused, and she sensed a force about him, a purpose and determination that surprised her. It seemed hard to believe, seeing him thus, that he could be the black sheep of the family.

"You love New Orleans, don't you?" she asked.

He smiled. "It shows, doesn't it? I love Louisiana too. And America. At least I remember that there is an America. Sometimes down here we get to thinking that only what we have in New Orleans matters."

"New Yorkers can be a little like that too," Lauré assured him.

"Come along," he said, "and I'll show you the French Market."

She held back for a moment longer. "What have you done that everyone so disapproves of?" she asked directly.

He stopped smiling, but he did not seem angry with her. He drew her hand through his arm and turned his back on General Jackson.

"If you really want to know," he said, "I'll tell you over a cup of coffee in the market."

She took one more look behind at the impressive sight of cathedral towers against a sunny blue sky, made a little bow to the general, and then went with Cole across the square toward the river.

"You can see the tops of ships above the town," he said, waving a hand toward the Mississippi. "The river is higher than the ground we're on, but you can't see it because it's hidden by the levees that keep it from flooding us out. There's the market over there."

Across the street stood a low building of pillars and arcades. She could hear the din of it, smell its rich and mingled odors, before she was well beneath the arches. This was a place of life and sound and color. The color of purple onions and cabbages, green lettuce, yellow squash, melons, pomegranates, bananas. The color and scents of water creatures too—live crabs and crawfish, frogs and turtles. Fowl cackled, parrots squawked, vendors shouted their wares or argued the price with some frugal Creole matron. Everywhere were to be seen the dark-skinned faces of Negroes, and even of Choctaw Indians. A separate flower stall added a vivid riot of color and perfume.

Already Mrs. Drummond, with Marie following, was considering purchases in her careful French manner. Cole let her know where he was taking Lauré, and then the two young people went to the little coffee stall at the end of the market and sat down at a small table.

Cole ordered cups of Creole coffee, and the man who served them poured it *au lait,* half milk and half coffee from two separate pots at one time. There were delicious honey cakes too, and piping hot rice cakes called *"calas,"* such as vendors sold in the streets. The Orleanian, with his French heritage, knew how to eat.

Lauré sipped the coffee and nibbled a cake. "Tell me now," she said.

"I almost hate to," Cole admitted. "I can't do nearly as

well as Jessamyn, and after her's my story is going to seem pretty tame. The problem has risen because my father wants me to go into his bank and live a safe, planned life as a proper son should. But banking's not for me. I want to be a schoolteacher."

"So?" Lauré said. "Is that all? What's wrong with that?"

"I suppose my father would accept it better if I were willing to become a university professor and attain a certain prestige and dignity. But I don't want that either."

"What is it you do want?"

A little girl had stopped beside their table in the open-air enclosure. A neat child, though plainly dressed. She stared at them round-eyed, and Lauré was about to offer her a cake when her mother called in French and she turned and ran back to her.

"That little girl's a Cajun," Cole said. "The word comes from 'Arcadian.' The Arcadians were among the earliest settlers in Louisiana, and Cajuns are still to be found living almost in the old ways, still speaking French. They don't live in New Orleans, but in their own part of the state. Some of the children manage to get a little education, through the church—the boys at least. Nothing much is done for the girls. There are also outsiders coming in by the hundred to buy land all through Louisiana—coming here from other states and bringing their families. For them there are no schools to speak of, and only a few teachers are willing to go to such outlying parishes—in Louisiana a parish is the equivalent of a county elsewhere. You can see why my father and mother are upset because this is what I want to do. They feel I'll be lost. To their way of thinking, I'll make nothing of myself."

Lauré nodded thoughtfully. "I can see why they would feel that way. Why is it you want to do this? I don't mean just because there is a need—but why *you?*"

He crumbled the cake on his plate absently. "I suppose I have a queer notion that I want to do something that matters to me. I don't mean that being a banker is of no consequence. But there are others who can do that work. This is the thing that challenges me. I'm sorry it makes my family unhappy, but I've got to go my own way. I've been down there recently going through some of the country places. Education is desperately needed."

"It's a little like the way I've wanted all my life to go on the stage," Lauré mused. "Nothing anyone can say will ever change that. And I have the right to choose."

He stirred his coffee and studied her soberly. "Yes, I suppose that's true," he said and then fell silent, lost once more in his own thoughts.

How different he was today from that time in the library, or even at the soirée. There was nothing bantering about him now, and he was no longer being highhanded, or bent on teasing. He did not treat her as Marcel had, like an attractive girl who would have nothing but flirtation on her mind. He talked to her as to someone who was an equal and might understand his problem. If only he would stay like this, she might find in him a friend, she thought.

He looked up suddenly, then spoke to her in an undertone. "Don't turn now to look. But a choice of action must be made. Arcadie and your grandmother are coming through the market. If you stay quietly where you are, they may never see you or know you are here. If we leave now, we will run into them."

Lauré suppressed the desire to turn her head, but her decision came instantly. She knew that just as she had felt the pull of that house on Royal Street, she felt now an urge to force the issue and come face to face with her grandmother.

"Let's leave and meet them," she said quickly.

Cole caught her by the wrist as she would have risen. "Wait! Are you sure you want this? 'Cadie is impulsive—she's sure to give your identity away. But Madame Beaudine may very well snub you. She may walk by without speaking. Do you want to risk that?"

A flush came into Lauré's cheeks, and she rose from the table, drawing her hand from his. "I don't see why she should snub me. It was not I who made the past."

He did not try to detain her, and they walked out of the coffee stall together and stood on the banquette, full in the path of the girl and the elderly woman who were coming toward them. Both were looking at the foodstuffs they passed, and Lauré had a chance to observe them before she was recognized. She spent no more than a quick glance on Arcadie's bright face—her interest was all for Madame Antoinette Beaudine.

Like her two spindly sisters, whom Lauré had seen during her first days in New Orleans, the old lady was dressed entirely in black, except for a white cameo brooch she wore upon her bosom. But she had not shriveled with age—her skin was smooth, with remarkably few wrinkles and only a little sagging at the throat. Her figure well corseted, was still handsome and full, her spine straight, her small graceful head held proudly high. In her right hand she carried a cane of black ebony, with a gold knob at the top. If she used it for support, that fact was not evident. One had a feeling as she pointed toward a succulent crab, or thumped the flagstones with it, that she used it for emphasis, that in a sense it was the scepter with which she ruled her Creole world.

The two turned from the market and came toward Lauré and Cole. Lauré saw Arcadie's eyes light, saw her quick smile. Then the girl glanced anxiously at her grandmother and hesitated. But Madame Beaudine had recognized Cole and she came toward him.

"Good morning, my boy," she said. "And how is your mother during this busy Carnival season? Well, I hope?"

"Very well," said Cole, and turned to Lauré. "May I present—" he began, but something in the old woman's expression stopped him.

She had noted his companion now, and the faint smile left her lips, the proud head lifted a notch higher. Lauré was aware of deep-set dark eyes studying her face, seeing every detail of it. Words froze in Lauré's throat. She dared not speak in the face of that scrutiny, though it made her a little angry.

When she had satisfied herself in her study, Madame Beaudine nodded to Cole and turned away. "Come, Arcadie. Let us go home."

Close to tears, Arcadie threw Lauré an unhappy backward glance as she followed her grandmother. Lauré could only stare after them blankly as the two crossed the street through busy traffic and moved toward Jackson Square. She was trembling with an anger born of hurt, but no less furious for that.

"Who does she think she is?" she cried to Cole. "How dare she treat me like that? She's ridiculous and impossible!"

"Calm yourself," Cole said curtly. "I warned you this might happen. And she's neither ridiculous nor impossible. She has simply acted according to her own code. You have to allow her that right."

"Then it's a foolish, impossible code!" Lauré cried, her voice choking.

"By now," said Cole, unruffled, "you have a good part of the market staring at you, and quite a few of those present know exactly what has happened."

She turned her indignation upon him. "As if I care! I'm going to find a way to pay her off—for my father as well as for me. I'm going to—"

Cole turned away from her. "If you're going to have a tantrum in the middle of the French Market, I hope you will excuse me for going back to my mother."

His words were like a dash of icy water in her face. She whirled away from him, looking for his mother and Marie. He came after her, moving in his own good time, and by the time they found Mrs. Drummond, Lauré was in control of herself. She said nothing of the encounter to her hostess, but she could hardly wait to get home and report what had happened to her father.

8. An Invitation and a Summons

WHEN they returned to the Drummond house, Lauré went straight to her father's room. The door stood open, and she found him sitting on the side gallery in the brisk, bright sunshine, a book upon his knees.

"Come join me," he called when he looked up and saw her. "Tell me how you liked the Vieux Carré and the

French Market."

Now her indignation was ready to spill over, and she could not stand still, but paced the length of the gallery as she spoke.

"I saw the Beaudine house," she told him. "And in the market we met your mother."

He closed the book, forgetting to mark the place. "How did this happen?"

She whirled about at the end of the gallery and came angrily back to him. His face was grave and attentive as she told him in detail exactly what had happened, but when she finished, his first words were unexpected.

"How did my mother look?" he asked.

She was still choking with indignation, and an impulse seized her. Never had her father permitted her to act anything out for him, but here was an opportunity. She would show him just how her grandmother had looked.

Impudently she thumped the ground with an imaginary cane and moved grandly toward her father. Then she looked him up and down haughtily before walking away with her head held high. It was all done in pantomime, and she knew her mimicry was good. A trace exaggerated, perhaps, but perfectly recognizable. She had given him a clear enough picture of Madame Beaudine's behavior so that he would be rightfully indignant at her treatment of his daughter.

His reaction astonished her. Jules Beaudine dropped his book to the floor and stood up.

"I do not care for such disrespect toward my mother," he said, his voice chill with disapproval. "It was not easy for her, I think, to give up her youngest son to the stage. But she had a right to follow my father's lead if that is what she

98

wished to do. Mimicry is a cheap thing. I hope you will never use it against her again."

Lauré stared at him, taken aback. "A cheap thing? But you use it all the time on the stage. And she was being cruel and unkind without any real cause."

"I am an actor, not a mimic," he said coldly. "The mimic catches only the outward semblance of a human being. An actor presents a character from inside—he becomes that character. You, my dear, hardly know enough to become a woman like Antoinette Beaudine. Never let me see you ridicule her again."

Lauré turned away from him, stung to the quick, feeling that he had used her unjustly, condemned her unfairly. Never before had he spoken to her in such clear disapproval, and his words left her trembling.

He let her go without calling her back, and she went down the hall to her own room. There she flung herself on the bed and wept out of confusion and misery. No one understood in the least the disturbing emotions she had experienced this morning. First, that glimpse of the Beaudine house and the strange longing that had risen in her at sight of it. A longing to see the place where her forebears had lived. Indeed, that longing had been the spur that had made her stand up and face her grandmother, hoping against hope that she would be accepted for her own worth.

And then there was the way Cole had been suddenly critical of her loss of temper, and now her father had condemned her effort to show him how his mother had behaved toward her.

She was still sitting there drenched in her sense of hurt and injustice when Jessamyn, home for noon dinner, came tapping on her door.

"Not now," she called to the child, but Jessamyn was persistent.

"Something has come for you by special messenger," she called through a crack in the door. "I know what it is, and it's terribly exciting. Do let me come in."

"Oh, all right," said Lauré surrendering to the inevitable.

Jessamyn eyed her with interest. "You've been crying, haven't you? Your nose is all pink. But never mind—this will cheer you up."

She extended an envelope of rich creamy paper, and Lauré took it without interest. She did not believe she would feel cheerful again for some time. Jessamyn brought a nail file from her dresser, and Lauré slit the envelope and drew out the engraved contents. It seemed to be an invitation, and she studied it doubtfully. Apparently she was being invited to a ball of some sort, and there was another, smaller card enclosed. When Jessamyn saw this she pounced on it excitedly.

"That's a call-out card, Lauré! You've been invited to a Carnival ball, and you've had a call-out too! Wait till I tell Mamma—!"

Lauré caught her by the hand. "Don't go rushing off. What do you mean—a call-out?"

Jessamyn turned back with an exaggerated air of patience, like an adult explaining something simple to a stupid child.

"This is the same ball that Mamma and Papa and Cole are invited to. And your papa too. It's one of the important ones. And the call-out means that a member of the krewe will have you called out on the floor to dance with him. It's a

100

very special honor. Only a few girls can be chosen."

Lauré examined the contents of the envelope again. "But it doesn't even say who is inviting me—only the name of the krewe."

"Of course not, silly! That's a secret. He'll be masked when you dance with him, and you may not know even then. But someone has picked you out because he likes you. Do come along and show Mamma."

Thus persuaded, and beginning to be interested in spite of herself, Lauré carried the invitation to Mrs. Drummond, who was in the dining room looking over the table.

Mrs. Drummond too seemed impressed and excited. She caught Lauré to her in a quick little hug.

"How marvelous! We couldn't hope for anything nicer to happen. And it's most unusual at this late date. In fact, the only way it could happen is by special permission of all the krewe. Perhaps some other girl who was invited couldn't attend and her invitation has been turned back to the krewe. So the man who invited her has been permitted to ask someone else. Who do you suppose it could be, Lauré?"

Lauré started to shake her head, when Cole, whom she had not noticed, spoke from the dining room doorway.

"Marcel Duval, I'm willing to bet," he said. "Years ago his father was Rex, and Marcel undoubtedly belongs to a krewe."

Lauré's father came into the room to see what the buzz of excitement was about, and Mrs. Drummond explained what had happened. He smiled at Lauré proudly, and she knew she had been forgiven for her offense in mimicking her grandmother. To her father also, the Carnival honor was clearly important.

"How fortunate that your new gown is nearly ready, Lauré," Mrs. Drummond said. "I think it will be suitable for the occasion. This is the most exciting thing that has happened in this house for a long while."

Cole glanced at Lauré curiously. "Somehow you don't look in enough of a feminine dither."

"I'm dazed," she said. "If it really is Marcel, he's being very kind—" She broke off, not knowing what else she could say. There was something almost disapproving in Cole's scrutiny, and it made her uncomfortable. After all, the matter was none of his concern. She was tired of being regarded critically by Cole Drummond.

Mrs. Drummond invited them to the table, her thoughts running on with a hundred details concerning the ball, and her tongue keeping up with them. Everyone seemed pleased except Cole. He ate his dinner absently and let the chatter flow over and around him. Once, just to get him to come back to the scene, Lauré asked him a direct question.

"You're going to the ball too, aren't you?"

"I'm expected too," Cole said, with one eye on his mother. "But aside from that, I think now that I might as well see the show. A blond Yankee with a call-out card should make something of a stir."

Jules Beaudine was not amused. "My daughter," he reminded Cole, "was born in New Orleans, and she has a Creole father."

"I'm sorry, sir," Cole said, but Lauré suspected that he wasn't. He still thought of her as a Yankee.

The big week of Carnival that culminated in Mardi Gras was to fall in March this year and was now only ten days away. Apparently a thousand things must be done before that time. Mrs. Drummond spent hours instructing Lauré on the conventions of the ball she was to attend, and on the responsibilities and privileges of being a call-out.

By now everyone in New Orleans seemed to be caught up in the mounting excitement. Hundreds of visitors would flock in from out of town. The hotels would be filled and merchants would grow hurried and harassed. To an outsider, it might seem strange that the entire population of a city should be so affected. But for those born to the spell of Carnival, the magic was taken for granted and everyone gave himself willingly to the tide of gaiety.

Behind the scenes, as Mrs. Drummond explained, all sorts of mysteries were going on. For a year the various krewes had been planning their parades, building their floats in secret dens in Calliope Street, each group guarding its plans from all others. The kings and queens had been chosen in the early fall and notified at Christmas time, though the kings of most krewes remained masked and their identities were supposed to be kept secret. Only Rex, king of all the Carnival, wore no mask, and his edicts and announcements were already appearing in the newspapers. The queens could be their beautiful selves and wore no masks at all.

A few days after Lauré had received her invitation, an unexpected caller arrived by carriage at the Drummond house. Arcadie had come especially to see her cousin.

"Grand-mère has sent me," she said breathlessly, as she ran up the steps and greeted Lauré. "Is there somewhere we can talk?"

Lauré took her into the library and closed the door. Arcadie seemed nervous and apologetic, as if she did not know exactly how to deliver the message she had brought. At the mention of Grand-mère 'Toinette, Lauré stiffened to resist further hurt.

Arcadie chose a straight chair and seated herself, her hands clasped tightly together.

"I—I do not know how to tell you this after—after what happened at the French Market," she said. "I asked Grand-mère to write what she wished in a note, but she would not do so. She said I must tell you myself."

"Then tell me," Lauré said. "Whatever it is, I won't blame you."

"*Merci*—I thank you," said Arcadie faintly. Then she gathered up her courage. "Grand-mère wishes you to come to see her."

Lauré stared. "She—wishes to see me? But why—after the way she snubbed me at the market? And why should I go?"

"I feared you would feel this way," Arcadie sighed. "Yet I have the great hope that you will do this thing and come to the Vieux Carré."

"But why?" Lauré repeated. "Why should I risk her further rudeness?"

"Oh, she would never be rude to you if you came as her guest!" Arcadie cried.

"But what made her change her mind?" Lauré asked. "Why should she pretend I didn't exist one moment, and then ask to see me the next?"

Arcadie shook her head helplessly. "This I do not know, but please come, Cousin."

"When does she want to see me?"

"This afternoon—now. Her carriage is waiting. I am to

fetch you to the Vieux Carré and bring you home later."

Lauré sat very still for a moment and let the tide of a strange excitement flow through her. This was the opportunity she had longed for—why not grasp it, lest it never come again? But first she must tell her father. She left Arcadie in the library and went upstairs to find him.

He took the news with a show of interest. "Go, by all means," he told her. "It is the first step, and fitting that it should come through you, who are her granddaughter."

She studied him thoughtfully, searching his lean, expressive face which could, nevertheless, conceal so much.

"This is why you came to New Orleans, isn't it?" she said.

For once he neither acted nor concealed, but answered her simply, tenderly. "This is why I came to New Orleans. It is my mother, always, who has drawn me back, even when I resisted, even when I knew she would not see me. Help me to make my peace with her, Lauré."

It broke her heart a little to have him make the request so humbly, and she was not at all sure that she could fulfill it. But when he drew her to him and kissed her cheek, she remained close to him for a moment, wondering if he dreamed how greatly she longed for his affection.

Arcadie was delighted and relieved when she came downstairs with her hat on, ready to go. In the carriage Lauré told her cousin about the invitation to the ball and the call-out card it contained. Arcadie's reception of the news was glowingly appreciative.

"How fortunate you are, Lauré!" she said. "I feel such a child to be only seventeen and left out of all these wonderful things. But next year I will make my debut at the opera and then perhaps I too—"

"At the opera?" Lauré puzzled.

"That is the Creole custom," said Arcadie. "Of course I have been to the French Opera House many times, but always a young girl must sit well back in a box. Not until she is eighteen does she sit at the front—being thus presented to society. It is very exciting. Young men who admire her may come to the parlor behind the box during intermission and present her with flowers and bonbons. If many come, she is a success. It is frightening as well as exciting—lest no one should come."

"I don't think you need to worry." Lauré smiled, watching the pretty, animated face of her little cousin. "Will you go to balls next year too?"

"Oh, I hope so!" Arcadie cried. "Then perhaps I too will receive a call-out card, if someone admires me enough."

"More than one, I should think," Lauré assured her. "But is there some special young man you'd like to receive one from?"

Arcadie hesitated for a moment, and Lauré remembered hearing how well chaperoned a Creole girl must always be. Arcadie's face dimpled and she laughed softly. "There is one—yes. You have already met him. His name is Marcel Duval."

Startled, Lauré said nothing. Beside her in the carriage, Arcadie fell into a daydream that left her face shining. Marcel? Lauré thought, remembering his flattery, his ardent words. But of course she had not believed him. Such things meant nothing in the South, where every girl expected such attentions from a man. Even if Marcel were behind the call-out card, the invitation still meant nothing. After all, he must wait another year before Arcadie would be old enough for his invitation.

"He lives next door." Arcadie spoke softly, dreamily. "His father is Grand-mère's attorney. In the course of working for his father, Marcel comes to our house often. As a child I played with him, and our families are good friends. Perhaps when I am old enough a marriage will be arranged."

Lauré listened uncomfortably. What if, in the meantime, Marcel should lose his heart elsewhere? Not that it would happen as far as she was concerned, of course. The very thought was absurd.

"We are nearly home," Arcadie said, and Lauré put the thought of Marcel from her mind as the carriage approached the tunneled entrance to the Beaudine house.

9. *Cameo Necklace*

FADED orange brick in a herringbone pattern paved the arched tunnel that led from the banquette to the inner courtyard. When Arcadie would have hurried ahead, Lauré put a hand on her arm.

"Don't rush," she pleaded. "I want to see everything."

Arcadie gave her a quick look of understanding. "But certainly! I have lived here all my life, so I take this house for granted. You are seeing our family home for the first time."

Strangely, there seemed to be offices on one side of the tunnel on the ground floor, and an antique shop on the other.

Arcadie saw her curious glance. "We have always been crowded for space in the Vieux Carré, and since the lower floors are apt to be damp, we use them for offices and shops. Our living quarters are upstairs."

Lauré paused at the edge of the open courtyard and looked about the sunlit expanse with pleasure. A small iron fountain, its rim edged with flowerpots, sent up a spout of water in the center of the paved court. In patches of earth grew bamboo trees, slender and feathery, broad-leaved banana plants, flowering vines, and green bushes. Galleries reached around on three sides, while a vine-covered brick wall closed in the rear of the court.

"Come, Lauré," Arcadie whispered. "Grand-mère will think it strange that I do not bring you upstairs to her at once."

The enclosed stairway curved gracefully, and Lauré followed her cousin to the second floor, her heart beating quickly now, her breath coming fast. The room into which Arcadie led her was a high-ceilinged parlor, opening on a gallery overlooking the court. Beyond lay a second parlor, dim and shuttered like Aunt Judith's parlor back home in New York. But it was in the brighter room that her grandmother waited for Lauré. The two aunts were nowhere in sight.

As she followed Arcadie in, she had a quick glimpse of rosewood furniture, a spinet in one corner, a small fireplace with a marble mantel, and above it a portrait that commanded the room. But she had no time to study the face in the picture—it was her grandmother's living presence that drew her.

Madame 'Toinette Beaudine sat straight in her chair, without deigning to touch her spine against its back. She wore black, as before, but today her silvery hair was revealed, drawn simply back from a central part—unfashionable in this day of pompadours, but for her dignified and becoming. The same pale cameo brooch, finely carved and set in yellow gold, fastened the high black-lace neck of her dress, and in her ears were small jet earrings which twinkled and danced when she moved her head. Before her was the ebony cane, set as straight as her spine, one blue-veined hand clasped upon its shining gold knob.

All these things Lauré saw as if in a picture, yet her true attention went at once to her grandmother's face, to the deep-set eyes, the unsmiling line of her mouth.

"Grand-mère, I wish to present Lauré Beaudine," Arcadie murmured formally. Then, sounding a little frightened, she added, "Do you wish me to leave you alone, Grand-mère?"

The gold-headed cane dipped slightly in Arcadie's direction. "*Attends ici,*" the old lady said. "You may wait here, 'Cadie." But her attention did not waver from Lauré.

Arcadie withdrew to sit quietly in a corner, while Madame Beaudine rose and crossed the room to stand before Lauré.

"*Bonjour,* my child," she said gravely. Her words, her intonation were even more French than Arcadie's. She spoke English as if she knew the language well but did not use it often.

Lauré took the small, fine-boned hand that was offered her and responded to the greeting. She expected either the casual conversation one might offer a guest or some explanation of why she had been summoned to this house. Her grandmother, however, gestured toward the portrait over the mantel.

"Do you recognize that portrait?" she asked. There was no warmth in her tone. It remained reserved, yet not unkind.

Puzzled by the question, Lauré studied the picture. Why

should she be expected to recognize a portrait in this house?

A man's face looked down upon her from the oval gilt frame—a face the artist had portrayed in middle age. The eyes were dark, and thick dark hair swept back from the forehead. A mustache trimmed the upper lip, concealing the mouth to some extent, but the stamp of resemblance was clearly there in the painted face. It came to her suddenly. The man in the picture bore a strong resemblance to her father.

"Is it my grandfather?" she inquired, keeping her tone as reserved as that of the old lady.

Madame Beaudine nodded. "How did you know?"

"Because of the resemblance to my father," Lauré said.

Her grandmother lifted the cane and gestured with its knob. "Stand there before the mirror. *Voilà!* Tell me now what you see."

Again Lauré obeyed and looked wonderingly into her own face. The resemblance leaped out at her doubly. She looked even more like her grandfather than did Jules Beaudine.

"*Vraiment*—but truly, you are a Beaudine," her grandmother said. "Except for your nose, perhaps, and that is mine. A good Fortier nose. You see how it is that I had no need for young Cole Drummond to present you. In spite of that pale hair, your face spoke to me at once."

Lauré stiffened, remembering the painful encounter in the French Market. "Then why did you turn away?" she asked boldly. "Surely that wasn't necessary."

Madame Beaudine returned her direct gaze. "Yes, it was necessary. If I had not walked away at once, I might have made an emotional scene there in the market place. Do you see that it might be unnerving to come suddenly upon the face of my beloved husband—a face that could belong only to his grandchild? His and mine."

She had not considered it like that, Lauré thought, and felt her resistance begin to fade.

"Come—let us sit down and talk a bit." Her grandmother motioned to a chair facing her own. When they were both seated, the old lady bent her penetrating gaze upon Lauré again. "It is, perhaps, not necessary to visit the sins of the father upon the child. It is possible, is it not, that we two might become acquainted?"

"I don't know," Lauré said carefully. None of this was going as she had imagined it. But she could not let her grandmother's words pass without defense. "I don't think my father was wrong in choosing what he wanted to do. In fact"—a hint of warmth came into her voice—"I feel that you and his father are the ones who have been cruel and without feeling or understanding."

Dark eyes widened in shadowed sockets. "You do not feel, then, that it is a sin for a child to defy the counsel of his parents, to turn upon them and choose a course that does not please them?"

"My father has proved that he was right," Lauré said. "He is reckoned among the great of his profession."

A soft gasp came from Arcadie in her corner, but Lauré faced her grandmother's gaze without faltering. To her surprise a faint smile lifted one corner of the old lady's mouth.

"So you are a rebel also, like Jules? Of course, my son would go far in whatever he attempted. He is like his father in that. But I do not wish to speak of him. What of you? Are you affianced as yet?"

Lauré shook her head. "I'm not, and I don't want to be."

"Indeed? And what else may a woman desire more than a suitable marriage and children?"

"I—I mean to go on the stage too," said Lauré, taking her courage in her hands.

The hand on the cane tightened, but Madame Beaudine gave no other sign of emotion. "Your father wishes this?"

"No, he doesn't. But I wish it. And I will find a way to do what I wish."

"I can see," said her grandmother tartly, "that you have not had the bringing up of a Creole lady. No properly brought up young lady would assert herself in such a manner. This is to be regretted. I wonder if it is too late to mend so unhappy a state. A woman of good breeding does not belong upon the stage."

Lauré sat in silence, staring at the ceiling. She saw that the chandelier, all adrip with crystal, hung from the center of an elaborately designed plaster medallion, and she studied the lacework of the medallion as if her life depended on it, so that she would make no further heated retort.

Arcadie spoke appeasingly from her corner in an effort to lead the talk along pleasanter lines. "Grand-mère, Lauré has been in New Orleans only a short time and has appeared at only one soirée, yet she has received an invitation to a Carnival ball—and a call-out card, as well!"

"Is this so, my child?" The old lady's face brightened, and Lauré almost smiled to herself. Even her stern Creole grandmother was apparently not beyond the spell of Carnival.

"Grand-mère would surely have been a queen, if she had not married so young," Arcadie added quickly.

Grand-mère acknowledged this with a gracious nod of agreement and then spoke again to Lauré: "Stand up, if you please. Let me see you walk across the room."

Surprised, Lauré rose and did as she was told. She remembered to use her graceful stage walk as she crossed the room, turned slowly, and returned to her grandmother's side. The old lady nodded her approval.

"You move with suitable grace, at least. Tell me how you will dress for this occasion."

Lauré described the frock of forget-me-not blue satin that was emerging so beautifully under Miss Willis' skillful fingers. Her grandmother listened to every detail with concentrated attention, nodding thoughtfully now and then.

"Blue will become you with your fair hair and coloring. It is too bad you are not more the Creole type, but you will make a great stir by contrast. Arcadie, fetch me, if you please, the jewel case from my room."

Arcadie flew to do her bidding and was back at once with a box of dark-red velvet and a small gold key. Grand-mère took the box upon her knees and opened it with loving fingers. In the velvet-lined trays Lauré saw the sparkle of gems, and she was aware of Arcadie looking in the manner of a small child before a treasure chest.

"Many of these are heirlooms," Grand-mère said, her fingers lingering briefly over a diamond brooch, a sapphire bracelet, an emerald ring. But the necklace she lifted from its tray contained no precious gems, though it was as beautiful as anything Lauré had ever seen. Grand-mère held it up against her black satin bosom, where it was displayed to good effect.

From a slender strand of fine, braided gold hung five

small cameos, graded in size from the largest in pale lavender and rose, to small ones in pink-tinted cream. Tiny blue enameled forget-me-nots in groups of three topped each cameo, fastening it to the chain.

"The cameos are of chalcedony, set in black onyx," Grand-mère said. "My husband bought them for me in Paris when I went there as a young bride. I've worn this necklace to many a grand affair at the French Opera, and to many a ball. I have always treasured it more than my diamonds."

"It's truly beautiful," Lauré said.

The old lady took one end of the necklace in each hand and held it toward her. "It is for you to wear for your first Carnival ball. A loan, of course."

Lauré was more moved than she had expected to be. "But I—I am afraid to borrow anything so precious—" she began.

"You do not call me Grand-mère," the old lady said, and put the necklace into Lauré's hands. "Let me hear you say the word. I wish it!"

The name did not come readily to her tongue. Lauré had a feeling that it was a name not to be spoken carelessly, or quickly, or too soon. Yet in the face of this loan, she could not do otherwise than force it to her lips, though it changed almost of itself as she spoke it.

"Thank you—Grandmother," she said.

Madame Beaudine did not look altogether pleased, but before she could remonstrate at the English word, Arcadie sprang to her feet and provided another distraction. She flew to the small rosewood spinet in a corner of the room and sat down upon a tiny stool that surely dated back to the days of hooped skirts.

"Listen, if you please!" she cried, and began to play a merry tune upon the keys.

All the severity went out of Grand-mère 'Toinette's face, and her black-shod foot began to tap the Brussels carpet.

"It is the Carnival song," Arcadie said over her shoulder. "Soon everyone in New Orleans will be singing it, in honor of Rex. 'If Ever I Cease to Love.'"

And as Lauré listened, her cousin began to sing gaily, charmingly, the nonsense words of the song.

> " 'If ever I cease to love,
> If ever I cease to love,
>   May fish get legs
>   And cows lay eggs,
> If ever I cease to love.' "

Grand-mère nodded to the tune, remembering. "I recall the time in '72 when Grand Duke Alexis of Russia, the czar's brother, visited New Orleans. At the time he was said to be in love with an actress who sang 'If Ever I Cease to Love' in a musical comedy. So to please the handsome Alexis, all New Orleans caught up the song and sang it to him at Carnival time. And we've been singing it ever since."

"There are so many variations—they go on forever," Arcadie said.

Now coffee was brought by a maid and served by Grand-mère, and Lauré sipped the thick black Creole mixture that seemed foreign and bitter to her tongue. For a little while longer Grand-mère spoke of matters that were far from serious. Then Arcadie found a box for the necklace and Lauré bade her grandmother good-by.

Nothing was said about a future visit, no mention was made of any message to her father. But as she drove away with the box clasped in her hands, Lauré knew she would return—if only to put the necklace once more into her grandmother's hands.

10. Carnival Ball

LATER that day in her room at the Drummonds', Lauré sat near a window overlooking the garden and thought about the visit to the Vieux Carré. When she had come home her father had wanted every detail, and she had tried to give him a faithful account. He had seemed pleased about the necklace, but had opened the box to look at it somewhat sadly.

"I can remember how beautiful she was when she wore it," he said. "It's fitting that she should lend it to her grand-daughter."

Yet Lauré sensed a questing in him that she could not satisfy, for she was not satisfied herself.

There had been no moment this afternoon when she had felt: This is my grandmother. This is the house where my family has lived back through the years. Instead of a surge of feeling that she had hoped for and half expected, all had seemed strange, including the old woman in black with her dark, sunken eyes and her gold-headed cane.

Had her grandmother been disappointed too? Had she too felt the lack of any real response between them? Yet she had made the gesture of lending her beautiful, treasured necklace to a granddaughter she did not know. Had the loan been an effort to bridge the gap that lay between them? If so, it had succeeded only momentarily.

Now the days flew along toward March, and Mardi Gras was almost upon them. There were many krewes that held balls but did not parade at all. Outside of the great krewes of Momus and Comus, only a few paraded in the days before Mardi Gras that year. On the night of one torchlight procession, the Drummonds invited guests less fortunately situated, and everyone sat on the front gallery upstairs, as if in a box at the opera.

Even Cole was there that night, though as usual he seemed to keep to himself. He was not unfriendly, but most of the time he seemed not to notice Lauré, and there was no way in which she could recapture the sense of companionship she had felt with him that day in the French Market when he had told her about his plans and desires.

Other young men had come to call after the soirée, among them Marcel Duval. Everything had been proper and well chaperoned by Mrs. Drummond, and there had been no way of questioning Marcel about the call-out card, even if he had been willing to answer. The thought of Arcadie's interest in him had continued to haunt Lauré but it would have been ridiculous to refuse to see him when he came to call. If he wished to be attentive, there was nothing she could, for the moment, do. But she felt uncomfortable in his company.

She had to admit, nevertheless, in all honesty to herself, that after the restrictions under which she had lived at Aunt Judith's, the company of almost any young man seemed pleasant and desirable. She enjoyed them all and gave her heart to none. Which was exactly as it should be, she thought with satisfaction. So why was it that now, when the Drummonds and their guests sat here on the upper gallery, watching for the parade to start down St. Charles Avenue, she should find herself glancing so often toward Cole—the one who paid no attention to her?

He stood behind the others at a side railing, not joining in the gay chatter. Perhaps not even listening to it. If she could have managed it, she would have liked to sit near him, to hear his comments on the floats as they came by. Was it that he found her unattractive, or that he disapproved of her because of her explosion that day in the market? She could not tell.

Without knowing it, she sighed, and then was caught up in the mounting excitement as the first burst of band music reached them, approaching down the wide avenue. Where was Arcadie tonight? Perhaps on the gallery of her own home on Royal Street, where the parade would eventually find its way. And perhaps Marcel had come over from next door and was with her tonight. Lauré hoped so. Not for anything did she want to give her little cousin pain.

The marvels of the night unrolled before the watchers along St. Charles—bands and marchers and mule-drawn floats. Tall Negroes, dressed all in white and carrying flambeaux to light the procession on its way, made capering escorts for every float. Red torch flames cast a weird orange light all about, bathing the elaborate floats of the king and his court. The theme of this krewe was the Court of Neptune, and the costumes were planned accordingly, aglitter with colored jewels like the bright fins of fish.

Crowds lined the banquettes on both sides of the street,

shouting and applauding, reaching out for the favors that were flung from the sacks of those riding on the floats. Cole suddenly left the group on the gallery, brushing past Lauré without a word. Watching, she saw him emerge below and run across the lawn in the flickering orange light. A moment later he was through the front gate, and she had lost him in the crowd on the banquette. She had the sudden rebellious wish to be a man so that she too could mingle with the crowd and watch the floats from the nearest vantage point, reaching for the trinkets that were cast abroad.

She did not note his return until he was suddenly beside her, breathless and laughing. "It was quite a struggle," he said, "but I caught a favor for you. Open your hand."

She obeyed, smiling up at him as he dropped a tiny gilded shoe into her palm. It was a cheap trinket, of no value, but she closed her fingers about it as if he had given her a treasure. This was a real token of Carnival, and it gave her pleasure to receive it from Cole. Yet, shortly after, he disappeared again and this time he did not return. She suspected that he had gone his way to Canal Street, where the greatest throngs were waiting, and she wished she might have gone with him.

That night when she went to bed she placed the little gilt shoe beside the chalcedony necklace in her dresser drawer, and did not see any contradiction in their proximity.

The shoe continued to be a good luck charm in the coming days, and two nights later she pinned it inside the bodice of her blue gown when she dressed for the ball. For luck, she told herself—because it stood for Carnival.

When she presented herself for her father's inspection that night, she had the pleasure of seeing his eyes light with approval. She knew her color was high and that the soft blue of her new gown set off her fair hair, just as her grandmother had said it would. The cameos in their black settings circled her throat, and she held in one hand a small ivory fan lent her by Celeste Drummond, who had carried it as maid of honor at a Carnival ball long ago.

Her father regarded her proudly, even perhaps tenderly. As they went downstairs together, he put an arm about her and held her lovingly. Once more she had the warm sense of having pleased him.

Cole had at length given in to his mother's insistence and he too was attending the ball tonight, though he was not altogether happy about it. As Lauré and her father descended the stairs, he stood in the hallway below, where once before she had wished him. But after a single quick glance in her direction, he seemed not to notice her appearance. Indeed, he seemed more interested in the fan she carried.

"So Mother lent you her precious Carnival fan, did she?" he said. "I hope you realize how highly you've been favored. You'd better move carefully tonight, what with your grandmother's necklace and my mother's fan."

"Stop trying to frighten me," she said. "I've had enough of that from Jessamyn. She's been telling me that krewe members have fallen off their floats and ended in a hospital, instead of at a ball. She has me terrified lest I get there and find that I'm not to be called out after all."

"In that case the skies will fall, I'm sure," he said dryly.

She had only meant to joke and she turned away from him, faintly annoyed. It was too bad that he was going along on this party, if all he could contribute was a dash of cold water. But she would not let him spoil her evening, and she shrugged the thought of him aside, so that she could concentrate on the marvelous time ahead.

This particular krewe was to give its ball in the old French Opera House in the Vieux Carré. By the time the Drummond party arrived, invited guests were presenting cards at the door, their names carefully checked in a master book file, lest an impostor steal in on someone else's invitation. The Drummonds were known and welcomed through the entrance.

The once-brilliant reds and golds of the famous opera house had faded to softer hues by now, but the great double staircase was as impressive as ever as they mounted it to the box which had been assigned to them.

"You young people must sit in front," Mrs. Drummond whispered as they entered the box, and Lauré found herself beside Cole in the front chairs, while Jules Beaudine and Foster and Celeste Drummond sat a little behind.

She looked about with the greatest interest. Over a good portion of the orchestra seats a removable floor had been placed, turning the section into a vast ballroom. Above the floor rose the curtained stage where the great Adelina Patti and so many others had sung their famous arias. Four tiers of balconies followed the horseshoe in graceful curves. Some of the boxes were open and hung with red-velvet curtains, while others had jalousies concealing them from view.

"Why do they have shutters?" Lauré asked Cole.

"Those are the *loges grillées*," he said. "Ladies who are in mourning, or who do not wish to make a public display of their presence, use those boxes. Needless to say, at Carnival time most ladies wish to display themselves."

"Why are you so prickly tonight?" Lauré asked. "You almost bite me when I speak to you."

He had been leaning forward on the rail of the box, watching the floor below, but now he turned his head and looked straight at her.

"I'm sorry," he said. "I suppose I have a bit of my father's impatience toward these affairs. But I ought to remember that you're here for your first Carnival ball and that it's a special occasion for you." He paused, and a quick smile crossed his face. "Right this minute you look about Jessamyn's age—all big eyes and excitement."

He could have said nothing that would please her less. She opened the ivory fan and leaned back in her chair, trying to give the effect of grown-up poise and boredom. But Cole only laughed at her haughty retreat.

"I like you better all eyes," he said. "Look over there—you're already the center of attention."

She glanced across the expanse of the theater to an opposite box and saw that several ladies had their heads together whispering, as they stared at the Drummond box.

"It's my father they're looking at," she told Cole. "Women are always silly about him."

"As men will be about you, I suppose," he said oddly. She laid the fan in her lap and stopped trying to pretend. "I think it would be fun to have several men silly about me, but so far it's never happened."

"What about Marcel?" he asked. "If he has sent you a call-out card—"

"I don't know that it is Marcel," she broke in. "Anyway, I'm only a substitute for the girl he invited first. And because Arcadie is too young for an invitation."

" 'Cadie is a dear," Cole said, and looked away from her. She wanted to ask if Marcel knew how Arcadie felt about him, but now the house lights were going down and the footlights were on, the stage alight behind the curtain. Carnival balls, it seemed, always began with elaborate tableaux. The curtains parted to a gasp from the audience, followed by a storm of applause as the opening scene, presenting the court of King Solomon, was revealed in glittering array. One tableau followed another after that, each one more beautiful, each one eliciting more applause than the one before.

Then the preliminaries were over, the house lights came on again, and maskers appeared on the floor below, where the krewe were gathering. The king and queen had been ensconced above the crowd on their thrones, and the revelry was about to begin. Lauré leaned forward eagerly to watch the maskers in their elaborate costumes and cloaks, each one with his identity concealed by a full face mask. Only the ladies they danced with would go unmasked.

Members of the committee moved about, calling out the names of ladies summoned for the first dance. Lauré tensed with listening, but she did not hear her name.

The procedure seemed strange to one not accustomed to the ritual. Only the krewe members were permitted on the floor, and they danced only with the ladies of their choice. Everyone else remained as an audience. A faint impatience stirred Lauré. What a shame that all this lovely music was going to waste, when she might have been dancing—even with Cole. But here she must sit and wait until her name was called.

She studied the maskers, searching among them for someone who looked like Marcel, but there were a dozen tall, slender men moving about the floor, and there was no distinguishing one from another behind the masks.

Beside her Cole yawned without restraint. "Why I came, I wouldn't know," he said. "Except that I'm bullied by my mother. And besides, I was curious to see how you'd take all this. How are you taking it, by the way?"

"I—I'm not sure," she said. "I wish I could be more a part of things."

Cole nodded. "For me the real Carnival is Mardi Gras. There's no sitting in boxes for that—you have to be a part of it. It's too bad you can't get into that."

"What do you mean?"

"I mean," he said, grinning at her, "that no young lady of *bonne famille*—good family, as the Creoles say—would go abroad masked and in costume on Mardi Gras."

He was watching her with something like amusement in his eyes, and she would have responded heatedly, but at that moment a voice from among those on the floor below began to bellow: "Mademoiselle Lauré Beaudine! Mademoiselle Lauré Beaudine!"

Lauré started, and Cole rose to draw back her chair. Mrs. Drummond bent toward her tenderly, sentimentally, and murmured words in French that Lauré did not understand. Mr. Drummond rose as she left the box, and Jules Beaudine gave her his arm proudly as he escorted her downstairs and turned her over to the committee member.

The man had been searching for her among other young ladies descending the stairs, and he hurried her across the floor before the dance music could start again, muttering that someday the committees would have sense enough to seat ladies who were present for call-outs on the main floor where they might be easily available.

Lauré's heart thumped a little as she moved through the glittering throng to her partner. It was exciting to be here, one of the chosen, one of the elite who could attend this wonderful ball. Cole's words about Mardi Gras were non-sense, of course. *This* was Carnival. Everywhere other girls in lovely ball gowns were being led toward their masked partners, and just as the first strains of the music began a tall man in the rich green and gold of an Eastern sultan, and wearing a gold turban, stepped forward to claim her. His face was hidden by a smiling mask with heavily painted eyebrows and puffy cheeks. But his voice when he spoke was Marcel's.

"Mam'selle Lauré," he said making her a formal bow, "you do me great honor." Then his arm circled her waist and she found herself swept away to the lilting strains of a Viennese waltz.

She danced gaily, breathlessly, always conscious of her partner and of the aura of mystery that surrounded him tonight, as part of Carnival. Yet she was aware too of the other whirling dancers, and of the watchers in the boxes above—those who could not dance, but came only to be an audience for this great affair. Once she lifted her head and gazed up at the Drummond box, to find her father's eyes upon her, as if he relished her success. Cole stood at the back of the box, and she could not tell whether or not he was watching.

It was all over too soon, and the girls who danced so light-heartedly returned to their seats. No girl would receive more than one call-out from any one man, but many of them would be called out by several. Lauré knew, however, that her own single dance, her little moment of glory, had come to an end.

"I will see you again before long," Marcel whispered. "Don't forget me!"

This was not the time to mention Arcadie's name, and she could only smile and nod. Before she left him, he gave her a small velvet box which she knew would contain the favor which it was customary to present to a call-out partner.

A few moments later she was back in the Drummond box and other names were being called for the next dance. Mrs. Drummond patted her hand as she joined them.

"Wasn't it lovely? And you looked beautiful, *chérie*. Now, then—show us your favor."

Lauré opened the little box and found in it a small brooch of pink coral and twisted gold. She felt uneasy about accepting so lovely a gift from Marcel Duval, though she knew that all ladies received favors from the men who invited them to a Carnival ball.

"Charming," Celeste Drummond murmured. "And was your partner really Marcel?"

Lauré nodded mutely as the brooch was passed around for the others to see. When it reached Cole he returned it to her without comment and slipped again into the chair at her side.

Lauré felt an urge to explain to him. "I know how Arcadie feels about Marcel—" she began.

Cole interrupted her casually. "There's nothing to keep him from asking you if he wishes. 'Cadie has no ties upon him. Don't feel guilty."

Before she could find an answer for this, he leaned toward her and whispered words the others in the box could not hear.

"You've had your Carnival glory now, and you've had Marcel's call-out. What about accepting an invitation from me?"

"What do you mean?" she asked.

There was surely a Carnival devil dancing in his eyes as he answered her.

"I mean an invitation to Mardi Gras. Come out with me Tuesday and have a taste of the real thing."

"You—you mean in costume?"

He nodded, his smile daring her. "And masked, of course. There's plenty of costume stuff in our attic."

"But your mother—would she—?"

"She would not," he said firmly. "If you tell her, it's all off. She would fling up her hands in horror. Your grand-mother would be appalled, and your cousin Arcadie would probably weep. As I've told you, a young lady of good family would never do such a thing."

Lauré glanced quickly about, but the attention of the others was on the dancers. No one was listening.

Cole leaned back in his chair, shrugging. "But of course you wouldn't dare. It was foolish to think you might have the courage—"

She faced him indignantly. "I won't do something just because someone taunts me about my courage. That's not fair!"

A little to her surprise he smiled, the mockery gone. "Good for you. You're right—it wasn't fair. I *am* feeling prickly. Let it go. It would have been fun to show you New

Orleans that way—and really perfectly safe. The crowds get a bit boisterous sometimes, but they're not rough. Never mind—of course it's out of the question."

For some reason she was more disturbed by his withdrawal of the absurd invitation than she had been at his taunt. At the back of her mind a vast curiosity about Mardi Gras was beginning to grow. Why could other girls go out in costume on that day, but not Lauré Beaudine? Cole, after all, would certainly feel a responsibility to look after his father's guest if she went with him. But there was nothing to do but push away these tantalizing thoughts and forget about the matter. In spite of what her own desires might be, she couldn't reward her father for bringing her down here by getting into some escapade that would reflect upon him and displease him if it were discovered.

Nevertheless, the thought was such an enticing one that the rest of the evening seemed a dull anticlimax of watching other girls dance when she could not be dancing herself.

The ball ended with a grand procession headed by the king and queen, who led their court away for a midnight supper. Mr. Drummond took his own party to supper at Antoine's, and once more it was very late when Lauré got back to her own room.

The last thing she did before she went to bed was to place three articles in a row upon her dresser. In the center was her grandmother's beautiful cameo necklace, next to it Marcel's coral brooch, and on the other side the little gilt shoe that Cole had caught for her from a passing float. She stared at the three sleepily for a long moment. Then she picked up the shoe and put it under her pillow before she got into bed.

Perhaps it would bring her pleasant Carnival dreams, she thought, and turned out the light.

11. Fat Tuesday Escapade

ON the evening before Mardi Gras, when everyone was out on the front gallery watching a parade, Cole signaled to Lauré and drew her into the house.

"At least you can help me choose my costume for tomorrow," he said. "Haven't you had enough of parades by now?"

This sounded like fun, and she went with him to the attic stairs at the back of the house and followed him up through a trap door in the ceiling. He had brought a lantern and some candles along, and when these were lighted a small area of the dim attic came to life. It was stuffy and warm up here, and dust had gathered in spite of Celeste Drummond's efforts to keep an orderly attic.

A number of trunks stood about, and Cole wiped the dust off one before he opened it. Inside had been stored garments that dated back through the years.

"My mother can never bear to throw anything away," he said. "There's everything here from Confederate uniforms to ball gowns that are out of style. I expect they'll all go to a museum someday."

He dipped into the trunk while Lauré watched, and brought out article after article. There were men's clothes as well as women's but each time when he held something up for Lauré's reaction, she shook her head.

"They're just clothes," she said. "Shouldn't you wear something that is really a costume?"

"With a little ingenuity, anything can be turned into a Mardi Gras dress," he told her, and dipped into the trunk again.

Lauré watched Cole with as much interest as she did the things he brought out of the trunk. What a contradictory person he was, with his solemn side—the side that made him want to be a country schoolteacher—often giving way to the fun-loving side.

"I've found it!" he cried. "Look here!"

Out of the trunk he had pulled a plain black dress, somewhat too full in the skirt for today's fashion, and was holding it up before him. Lauré stared at it, puzzled.

"But that's a woman's dress."

"Wait," he said. "Turn your back a moment."

She turned away until he called to her to look, and then she swung about to see that Cole had transformed himself into an old-fashioned Creole *tante*. When he pulled a black bonnet over his head, he could easily pass for Tante Sophie or Tante Gaby. With a little effort, he even managed to imitate their prim, dignified walk.

"But it would be no fun alone," he said. "There ought to be two of us to carry out the picture." He reached into the trunk and pulled out another black dress. "Try it on, Lauré Just for fun."

There was certainly no harm in trying on the dress. Like Cole she put it on over her clothes and did not bother to hook it up.

He laughed out loud at the picture she made, and tossed her a second bonnet to cover her blond hair.

"There's a mirror over here," he said. "Come have a look at us."

He moved the lantern so that it would light the long glass on a discarded *armoire,* and she stood beside him staring into the mirror. The sight of two genteel ladies peering out at her sent her into a gale of laughter. She was laughing so hard she did not hear her father's voice until he called up the attic stairs a second time.

"Lauré! Are you up there? You're missing a spectacular float that's coming down the street. What are you doing in the attic?"

Lauré stared at Cole in dismay. It would never do to have her father think she meant to go out in costume with Cole on Mardi Gras. But before she could find her voice, Cole called out to him.

"There's a better show up here, sir. Do come up and have a look." Then he whispered to Lauré, "Act your part!"

Jules Beaudine climbed the stairs briskly, while Lauré tried to think what to do. Not knowing whether she would be scolded again for being a mimic, she took a prim turn about the attic at Cole's side and returned for her father's inspection. To her relief, he burst into a roar of laughter.

"You'd make a fine Mardi Gras pair! Is that the costume you mean to wear tomorrow, Cole?"

"I might, if I could persuade Lauré to go with me," he said boldly.

Lauré froze. This was the worst possible thing Cole could have said. She started to speak, but her father waved his fingers at her to be still.

"Why not? It's a good idea. No one has truly lived until he has known the fun of a New Orleans Mardi Gras."

Even Cole looked startled. "You mean you wouldn't mind if Lauré went out with me tomorrow, masked and—"

"I can remember doing the same thing myself," the actor said, lost in reminiscence. "I couldn't have been more than seventeen at the time, though the young lady was a year older. But of course I couldn't permit my daughter to go off unchaperoned in your company, young man. Let's see if we can find another costume and we'll make it a trio. We might as well have three culprits, instead of only two."

He was amazing, this father of hers, Lauré thought in a surge of relief. Yet at the same time she had the faintly uneasy feeling that he was somehow not behaving exactly as a parent should.

The procession outside was forgotten as they searched the trunks for a costume suitable for Jules Beaudine. The discovery of a black-and-white checked vest gave him an idea.

"With this vest, I'll need only a few touches to get myself up as a Mississippi gambler," he said, falling delightedly into the spirit of the masquerade. "Here's an old bowler hat that will do, and I'll shop for a mask with a handsome mustachio. What would be more in keeping for Mardi Gras than two prim Creole ladies in the company of a flashy American gambler?"

Cole grinned his approval. "There is, however," he reminded them delicately, "the matter of our getting out of the house unseen in the morning. I'm afraid my mother would still not be pleased to have Lauré run with the masked crowds on Mardi Gras."

Jules Beaudine nodded. "A little deceit may be necessary. Mardi Gras is of course a holiday, so the family will probably sleep late. Suppose we get up before anyone else and make our escape in costume. I'll leave word that I've taken you off on a little jaunt. In my company it will all sound proper enough. They needn't know that Lauré is masking."

"Perhaps you'll be the one in trouble," Lauré told her father.

"It won't be for the first time," he said complacently. "Get out of those things now and smuggle them downstairs while I make sure the others remain on the gallery."

He disappeared through the trap door, giving them a last long wink before he vanished. Cole chuckled as he got himself awkwardly out of the dress.

"Do you know, I like your father better than I expected to. He hasn't forgotten what it's like to be young."

Lauré drew one arm out of a sleeve and then perched herself absently on the corner of a trunk. "Yes, he is fun, isn't he? But sometimes I wonder—" She paused because the thing she was wondering seemed vaguely disloyal. Was this another role her father was playing? Or was he just a bit irresponsible? She knew he liked to fly in the face of convention, and surely she ought to be glad of the fact, since it was giving her an opportunity to do, without blame, the thing she wanted to do. Why should a troubled feeling remain—as though she herself ought to make some other decision?

"You'd better hurry," Cole said, and held out his hand for the dress.

She got out of it quickly, and they rolled their separate costumes into bundles and started for the stairs. But just before Cole went ahead to help her down, he paused and looked at her thoughtfully.

"Something's worrying you, isn't it? Don't you really want to do this?"

"Of course I do," she said, not wanting him to think her

foolish and prudish, not wanting him to know that she sometimes doubted her own father just a little.

He reached up to take her hand as she started down the steps, and after she had reached the lower floor he held it for a moment.

"All right," he said, "don't tell me if you'd rather not. But don't worry about tomorrow. I'll try to keep both you and your father out of trouble."

She knew he was laughing at her again and she drew her hand quickly away. She took the rolled-up black dress to her room and hid it in a dresser drawer.

By the next morning, fortunately, all her uneasy feelings had vanished. She was wide awake and eager at the appointed hour, with not a misgiving on her horizon. When she had managed to get herself into the black dress—by good luck the hooks were all within reach—and had tucked her fair hair well under the concealment of the black bonnet, she stole downstairs to meet Cole and her father in the lower hallway.

Until the three conspirators were well away from the house, she half expected Jessamyn to wake up and discover them. But everyone remained asleep, and they hurried down St. Charles without being discovered. It was not difficult to find a small shop that sold masks on Mardi Gras, and Jules Beaudine bought one with a false mustache glued to the broad upper lip—a real mustache with ends he could twirl with bravado. Lauré and Cole chose identically prim elderly lady masks that fitted their costumes perfectly.

Already other early risers were abroad in costume in order not to miss a moment of this exciting day. Rex, the Lord of Misrule, was king, and within reason every man could do as he liked on Mardi Gras, his courage made great by the concealment of the mask that hid his true identity.

The three caught a mule-drawn car that took them down to Canal Street, where revelry had already begun. The street was hung with decorations in the purple, green, and gold of Carnival colors, and shop windows were gay with Carnival displays. In a small eating shop they breakfasted together on Creole *café au lait* and a *croissant* apiece. The crescent bun with its crisp, flaky crust tasted better to Lauré than anything she had ever eaten. Afterward, they put on their masks again and wandered out into the growing throngs.

Costumes ranged from the prosaic to the spectacular and imaginative. Red devils with horns and long spiked tails capered through the crowds playing good-natured tricks. There were clowns aplenty, characters from *Mother Goose*, and creatures from *Alice in Wonderland*. A young fellow dressed as the knave of hearts flung himself to his knees before Cole and beseeched the *"agréable"* Creole lady to elope with him. Jules Beaudine twisted fierce mustache points and ordered the fellow off. But it was all good-humored and all in fun.

At Mardi Gras time, Cole said, the phrase had it that you "became" a Mardi Gras—you really got into the spirit of the thing.

Now horse-drawn carts of every description were carrying maskers past in a colorful miniature parade that would eventually attach itself to the end of a real parade. With a Creole lady on either arm, the Mississippi gambler managed to get his charges across Canal Street and into the French Quarter.

Here they walked the narrow streets along with the Mardi

Gras crowds, enjoying the costumes and the capers, feeling themselves part of the gaiety. Never before had Lauré felt so great a sense of freedom and escape from the restrictions that surrounded her as a young lady in this last decade of the century. She could exchange greetings with strangers, laugh out loud, and waltz with her father on the banquette to the tune of a mouth organ played by a small hobo with a painted red nose.

The very essence of Mardi Gras was laughter and fun, and Lauré's spirits soared with the rest. In no time at all she was calling out, "Mardi Gras!" after strangers, as they did to her. She sang "If Ever I Cease to Love" with all her heart and voice, and kept picking up new words to the Carnival tune. Now and then she was aware of Cole watching her behind his mask, and once when she had whirled away from her father to do a bit of Virginia reel with a merry clown, he tapped her shoulder when she came back to them.

"Who would have thought a Yankee girl could turn into a real Mardi Gras?"

Again her father prickled at the word "Yankee." He turned his fierce mask in Cole's direction. "Don't forget that Lauré was born in New Orleans—that this is her home." Quite clearly he did not like to hear her called a Yankee, and that made Lauré laugh all the harder. For she was Yankee and Orleanian all rolled into one, and for the moment the mixture did not seem incompatible.

She gave no thought now to what Mrs. Drummond would think if she knew what was going on. By the time they got home, it would be too late for opposition, the deed would be done, and her father would have to talk them out of it. In this mood the morning rolled gaily along, until they all grew ravenous on laughter and excitement.

Restaurants in the Vieux Carré were crowded, but they managed to get into one, and Jules Beaudine ordered a satisfying Creole meal with jambalaya and red beans and rice. They ended with *café brûlot,* set aflame by the waiter as it was served to them.

It was in the restaurant, however, that they lost Jules Beaudine. They had, of course, removed their masks in order to dine, and Lauré had been startled when, near the end of the meal, a man had stopped beside their table to clap her father on the shoulder. If this were some acquaintance of the Drummonds—!

But it turned out to be a boyhood friend of Jules's, in the days when he had lived in New Orleans. The two were delighted to see each other and clearly had a good deal of catching up to do. When the newcomer invited Jules to his nearby rooms for a visit, Lauré's father looked at her like a small boy asking to be excused from a duty.

"You two won't mind, will you?" he asked. "I must confess my feet are a bit weary, and you young people can keep going for hours. Cole, may I trust Lauré in your keeping, while I go off for a good talk with Henri?"

Cole agreed readily, and Lauré was barely consulted. Before she knew quite what had happened, her father had paid the bill and Cole had promised to see her home safely himself, rather than to attempt meeting Jules again in the crowd.

When the two men had gone, Cole glanced at her in amusement. "You should see your face, Lauré! I can't say that I'm especially flattered. It's not so awful to be left alone with me, is it?"

"It's not that," she protested. "He—he shouldn't have gone off as carelessly as that!"

"You're being a stiff-necked little Yankee," Cole said. "Let New Orleans teach you how to have fun."

She couldn't explain to him how she felt. It wasn't because Aunt Judith would have been appalled at what was really a very innocent and harmless adventure. It was the light way in which her father had put aside all responsibility and gone his own way without the slightest twinge of conscience.

"I think," she said doubtfully, "that I don't understand New Orleans men at all. Not my father. Not you. Remember that day in the French Market when you told me about what you really want to do with your life? How does that fit in with this? How could you sound so serious about teaching in poor sections that need you, and yet act today as though you hadn't a serious thought in the world?"

He smiled at her. "Mardi Gras is the one time when we can fling off serious thoughts and be what we are not. Come along, Lauré—let's go back to it. It only lasts a little while, so let's get our fill of it."

They put on their masks and went back into the streets, to be caught up once more in the excitement. Forgetting her father and her momentary qualms, Lauré began to feel that it was more fun to stand elbow to elbow with the people—to whom Mardi Gras really belonged—than it had been to watch the tableaux from an exclusive box at the ball a few nights before. Cole had been right about Mardi Gras being truly Carnival.

The sun grew warmer and their masks became uncomfortable, and after a time, like others around them, they took them off, feeling themselves still sufficiently costumed. It would be necessary to get back to the Garden District in time for the evening meal, and they turned at last toward Canal Street, swinging their masks by their strings as they walked along, striding a little too freely now for the proper Creole ladies they represented.

Neither paid much attention to the fact that they had turned onto Royal Street, until suddenly Lauré heard a voice calling her name in astonishment from a gallery across the street. She looked up in justified alarm. There behind the iron lacework, where they could watch Mardi Gras comfortably, sat Arcadie and Madame 'Toinette Beaudine. Perhaps the old lady's eyes would not have observed them had it not been for Arcadie's impulsive recognition, but now Grand-mère rose and peered down at them from her balcony.

"I'm afraid we're in for it," Cole said in Lauré's ear. "It's all my fault. I should have watched where we were. What do you want to do?"

They had no choice in the matter. Grand-mère 'Toinette did not raise her voice to an unladylike pitch, but she beckoned to them firmly with a raised hand.

"We'll have to go in and see her," Lauré said.

Of all the encounters she would least have chosen under such circumstances, it was this one.

12. "If Ever I Cease to Love"

ARCADIE ran downstairs to let them in through the gate, and her expression was doleful. "I'm sorry," she told Lauré. "If only I'd kept still! But I was so astonished when I saw you, I could hardly believe my eyes. Grand-mère, is terribly upset. I'm afraid this is going to be quite painful."

Cole took Lauré's arm reassuringly as they went upstairs. He seemed less appalled than Lauré, but then, Grand-mère, 'Toinette was not *his* grandmother.

Lauré felt more uneasy over facing her grandmother than she would have believed possible. She tried to remind herself that what this woman thought did not really matter. Yet that strange tugging at her innermost being had begun again. No matter what her reason told her, her heart whispered that it mattered very much. It was a disturbing thing to so disappoint and anger her grandmother.

Once more Madame Beaudine waited in her parlor, and once more the gold-headed cane was in her hands. Her eyes were bright with displeasure, and her mouth was set in a firm line that boded no good to any who opposed her. She dismissed the frightened Arcadie with a glance, and Lauré was sorry to lose her cousin's friendly presence.

Grand-mère, greeted Cole briefly and then spoke directly to Lauré. "You will explain, if you please, the meaning of this disgraceful behavior."

Lauré sat down, though she had not been invited to. She didn't want to stand up like a small girl about to be scolded.

"You're mistaken about it's being disgraceful," she said, trying to sound calm and reasonable. "My father brought Cole and me downtown for Mardi Gras. A little while ago Papa met an old friend and we separated. Cole was about to take me home."

The old lady swept Cole with a scornful look, as he stood beside Lauré's chair. "Do you feel satisfied with yourself, young man—abroad in a woman's dress, mocking those who are your betters? And escorting a young lady of supposedly good name about the streets in the company of vulgar people?"

"I'm sorry you disapprove," Cole said, unabashed. "I value your good opinion, Madame Beaudine, and would be sorry to lose it."

"You have already lost it," she said tartly. "My son may know no better—life in the theater has clearly lowered his standards. But you are a well-brought up New Orleans boy and I am ashamed of you."

"You needn't be, Madame," Cole said gently. "At Mardi Gras New Orleans belongs to the people. Before long I hope to be teaching the children of just such people as you'll find abroad today. All good citizens of Louisiana. I do not consider myself above them."

Grand-mère's proud nostrils drew in as she sniffed her displeasure. "I had forgotten that you are willing to break your mother's heart, just as my son broke mine. But no matter—the fault for what has happened today is not yours. It is not even my son's." She looked at Lauré with an air of being quite sure where the main fault for the escapade lay.

"Grandmother, I really don't feel that—" Lauré began, but the old lady silenced her at once.

"Enough! Empty words will not help you. It is the lady, always, who is to blame when matters get out of hand. No real lady would ever think of allowing herself to be found in such a situation in the first place."

Lauré bit her lip. She mustn't get angry. "What *is* a lady, Grandmother?"

Madame Beaudine's dark eyes flashed with indignation. "No one who carries the name of Beaudine need ask such a question."

"I'm sure Lauré knows very well what a lady is," Cole put in. "But perhaps the definition changes from generation to generation. Perhaps other definitions are valid too, depending on the period in which you live."

Lauré threw him a quick look of gratitude. What a surprising person he was. There he stood in his ridiculous female costume—though at least he had removed the bonnet. Yet he was not ridiculous. He did not seem in the least embarrassed or ill at ease.

"Do sit down," said Grand-mère sharply, forgetting that she had not previously invited him to. "There will be less of you then to offend my eyes. You are implying, I suppose, that I am ancient and old-fashioned, that the principles of my girlhood have been deserted in this dreadful modern age?"

"You could never be old-fashioned, Madame Beaudine," said Cole gallantly. "But perhaps there was a day when you too rebelled from some ruling that you thought unfair, or—"

She stopped him. "We are not here to discuss my youth. Tell me, sir—what is *your* definition of a lady?"

Cole thought a moment, and his eyes were on Lauré. "I should think a lady would be one who could go anywhere and by her conduct be treated with respect. It seems to me that Lauré is that sort of lady."

Lauré was not sure she deserved Cole's words, but she was grateful to him for speaking them.

Grand-mère looked surprised, and it was possible that a faint quirk showed at one corner of her mouth.

Lauré saw it and quickly pressed the advantage. "What

you did as a girl *is* important. It's important because you can't judge us unless you remember what it was like to be young. Did you never, never break the rules?"

"Perhaps," the old lady said dryly, "it is because I remember all too well what it was like to be young that I wish to see the proper restrictions set upon a well-bred young girl today. However, I can assure you that I was guided by my parents in my youth, and later by the wishes of my husband."

Lauré glanced at her grandfather's portrait above the mantel. He must have been a gentleman to his very finger tips, and he would have had nothing less than a perfect lady for his wife. But it was Claude Beaudine who had sent Grand-mère's youngest son out of the house, never to return.

"Were the wishes of your husband always wise?" Lauré asked softly.

When her grandmother's eyes flashed like that and she looked proud and indignant, she was an extremely handsome woman, Lauré thought, but an even more formidable one.

"Your question is impertinent," Grand-mère said. "I can see that it is not you with whom I must deal at this point. I will have my carriage made ready to drive you both home. But something must be done to correct this matter. I shall write your father a letter. You may tell him to expect to hear from me."

What that meant, Lauré could not guess. After all, her father had thrown himself in with them on this escapade. He could hardly be expected to punish her for what she had done. At any rate, she had been firmly dismissed by her grandmother.

Grand-mère's carriage had to take a roundabout way to get out of the French Quarter and across Canal Street at its least crowded section. During the drive Lauré had the feeling that she was being sent home like a naughty child. She was sorry to have taken Cole away from his fun. He didn't seem to mind, however, and as they drove toward the Garden District he spoke about her grandmother with respect in his voice.

"She must have been very beautiful when she was young. My mother has a picture of her. For all that she was chaperoned to the teeth, more than one young Creole blade fell in love with her. Rumor has it that two of them fought a duel over her favor. I'd like to know more about that story!"

This gave Lauré an unexpected glimpse of 'Toinette Beaudine. It was reassuring to be with Cole, to listen to him talking as casually as though nothing serious had happened. And of course nothing really had happened. What did it matter, she asked herself again, if a prudish Creole grandmother disapproved of her? Her grandmother's world was far removed from that of the Lauré Beaudine who would someday be a great actress and live a life that would certainly shock Madame Beaudine far more than anything that had happened today. The realization helped her to relax a little and thrust the odd sense of disappointment away from her.

She fell to watching Cole as he talked. He had wriggled out of the black dress, which he'd worn over trousers and shirt, and had now flung it like a cloak about his shoulders to cover his shirt sleeves. How nice he was when he was friendly and kind, as he had been today.

He began to sing "If Ever I Cease to Love," and she joined him, humming softly, wishing she could recapture the carefree feeling of Mardi Gras.

When the carriage neared the Drummond house, Cole stopped it and they got out. He knew a short cut by way of the back lawn, and he managed to get Lauré unseen through a side door and into the house. All would have been well if Jessamyn had not come out of her room and spied them as they stole upstairs.

The child had no more than opened her mouth to exclaim, however, before Cole dived for her and put his hand over her lips, while he whispered urgently in her ear. Whatever he said quieted her, and though her eyes were big with excitement, she went back to her own room as though she had seen nothing out of the way.

"I told her this would make a wonderful plot for a novel and I would tell her all about it later, if she would say nothing to anyone about seeing us," Cole said as he saw Lauré to the door of her room.

She smiled and held out her hand to him. "Thank you for—for everything. I've had a wonderful time."

There was laughter in his eyes as he took her hand and went through the courtly gesture of kissing it in the French manner.

"I've had fun too. And, Lauré—don't ever worry about not being a lady. You are one. And I agree with your grand-mother—it's still something worth being."

He left her then, and she closed her door and got hurriedly out of bonnet and black dress. It was almost time for the evening meal, and she would be able to go down as calmly as though she had not been out enjoying Mardi Gras all day.

That is, unless her father spoiled everything and told Mrs. Drummond the truth. She didn't know if he'd come home yet, and he was so unpredictable.

However, instead of washing and dressing at once, she sat dreamily on the bed and thought about Cole Drummond. She thought about him with a pleasant warmth of liking. How strange that only a little while ago she was telling herself she did not like him, when now she was ready to admit that she liked him very much indeed! The Carnival tune came into her mind again and she hummed it softly, wordlessly.

After a while she got up as aimlessly as she had sat down, and wandered across to the mirror on her dresser. The face that looked back at her was ashine with something she had never seen in it before. It was not, after all, a terribly plain face. There was a glow in the eyes, a lift to the corners of the mouth—in fact there was upon it a look of enchantment.

She remembered the Lady of Shalott who had broken out of her spell and looked down upon the brave Sir Lancelot as he rode by. And that, sadly enough, had been the end of the Lady. Realization swept over her in a rush, and she stared at the girl in the mirror as if at a stranger.

"You've done it!" she cried softly. "You've done exactly what your father said you would do. You've taken one look and fallen in love with the very first man you've met in New Orleans!"

She stared at herself for a long, astonished moment. Then the first twinge of apprehension touched her and she turned from the mirror. How could she have been so foolish—when Cole was the last man in the world to be right for her? How could she think of him for a moment when she was going on the stage and he was to be a schoolteacher in some benighted Louisiana parish? It was sheer nonsense, of course—she wouldn't be in love with him, she didn't have to be. "If ever I cease to love," indeed!

"Go away!" she told the feeling crossly, and hurried to dress for the evening. No one had to be in love if she didn't want to be, she told herself, combing her hair with extraordinary care.

She went downstairs holding herself firmly in check. She would not so much as look in Cole's direction, she decided—and looked at him first of all as she went into the dining room. She was startled and dismayed by the sudden thudding of her heart, and by the betraying flush that swept into her cheeks. The others were already there, waiting for her. Her father gave her the sly wink of a conspirator, and seated her gallantly in her place. Mr. Drummond and Cole were listening to Celeste Drummond, and except for a brief turning of heads, no one paid any attention to her. Cole least of all.

As they took their seats at the table, the look of being far away was on Cole's face again, as if his thoughts were elsewhere. Back in the Mardi Gras crowd, perhaps? If he had ever seen Lauré Beaudine in his life before, there was certainly no way to tell it.

13. Banishment

THE days after Mardi Gras were strangely quiet. New Orleans had wound itself up to the final moment of sparkling climax, and then gone down with the limpness of a deflated balloon. Here and there a bit of tinsel clung to a shrub, a broken whistle lay in the gutter, a torn mask was swept away by the wind. Another Mardi Gras was memory. Only in the dens of Calliope Street was there a mysterious and secret activity as the krewes gathered to discuss their plans for the most wonderful Carnival that was ever to be held in New Orleans—the one for next year.

The weather grew a bit warmer, and the camellias and azaleas began to bloom. Birds sang in the gardens as the city prepared for spring.

The letter Madame Beaudine had promised to write did not come, and Lauré almost forgot about it. She had other things to think of by now. Mainly Cole. She did considerable pondering over whether or not the feeling she had about him was what novels and older people referred to as "love." If going hot and cold when Cole was near, if yearning for his attention and interest and thinking about him most of the time, whether he was present or not, was "love," then this must certainly be it. It was not very comfortable.

The sensation, she found, was not something that would go away when she dismissed it. What was worse, it made all other young men seem insignificant when measured beside Cole. It left her in happy misery. That is, she rather enjoyed the feeling, and yet was miserable at the same time because it was quite clear that Cole himself entertained no such yearnings toward her. Yet, perversely, she would not have given up her misery for anything. At least she had the wit to conceal her feeling from Cole. She sensed that a young man whose own emotions were not involved would not welcome a display of feeling on the part of a girl he scarcely knew existed. And, of course, she hid the way she felt from her father. She could imagine the mocking lift of his eyebrows if he were to suspect what had happened.

If this was love, then it was a lonely thing, and that seemed wrong. The love she had read about, for all its vicissitudes, was an emotion shared by two, or even sometimes by a triangle of three. It was not something one should have to brood about and grieve over alone.

After Mardi Gras, Cole went his own way again. Much of the time he was deep in study and preparation for the work he had set his heart upon. The gaiety of Mardi Gras had left him, and he paid little attention to Lauré, even when they were in the same room at the same time.

Into this burgeoning of love and springtime came the letter from Grand-mère 'Toinette to unsettle Lauré's world still further. It was addressed as the old lady had promised, to Jules Beaudine, and Lauré had warned him that such a letter might come.

Her father had been more distressed over her discovery by Madame Beaudine on Mardi Gras than he had ever been over the idea of the escapade itself. Indeed, he had been furious and explosive for all of ten minutes about Lauré's carelessness in walking down Royal Street past her grandmother's house. But her father's rages, as Lauré was learning, while they might go off like lighted firecrackers, never lasted for long and were quickly forgotten—by him at least—until they recurred again.

The letter sent him into the hallway shouting for his daughter. Lauré came running, and knew at once what was wrong when she saw the sheet of letter paper in his hand.

"Grandmother has written to you?" she asked.

His lean, handsome face was suffused with angry color as

he gestured Lauré into his room for a private talk. She followed him and sat down in a chair near a window, waiting unhappily for whatever was to come.

"You must have behaved very badly indeed that day *Maman* caught you masquerading," he said. "I find it hard to believe that your Aunt Judith taught you so little of good manners and the proper behavior of a young lady."

The fact that she knew he would shortly get over his anger never comforted Lauré very much at the time. While he might recover quickly and forget, the sharp things he said often lingered on to hurt her, wounding again as they returned to mind. Strange that he could be so kind and thoughtful at one time, and so very different at another. And how hurtful—when she longed so much for his love and approval!

"I don't believe I was rude to her, if that's what you mean, Father," Lauré said. "I didn't feel that I was doing anything wrong, and I had to stand up for my own position."

Jules Beaudine walked the floor of the room as if he stalked the boards of a stage, and his indignation did not abate.

"Listen to this!" he cried, and read aloud a portion of the letter.

"'Since my granddaughter clearly lacks the suitable training of a young lady of good family, I have decided that I must mend this sad matter. I wish her to come here for an extended visit. Perhaps it is not yet too late to teach her some of the graces and attitudes that have been neglected in her raising. Please send her to me as soon as it is possible.'"

Lauré listened in astonishment. What a highhanded,

dictatorial old lady she was!

"Of course I won't go," she said quickly.

"That is for me to decide," her father returned, as if he were quite accustomed to using the prerogatives of a father, instead of avoiding them most of the time.

With no more thought than her father had given to his own outburst, Lauré jumped to her feet. "Why should I go to her house to learn a lot of things that will never be of any use to me? She'll be worse than Aunt Judith, and I've had enough of that. None of these things will teach me what I really want to know—how to be an actress. You're the one who could train me for that, if only you would. If only you'd give me a chance!"

"No lady raises her voice at any time," her father said, raising his own voice, but saying nothing about gentlemen. "I can see that your head is still filled with foolish, stage-struck notions. This settles it. If anyone can take them out of you, *Maman* can. I shall ask Celeste to drive you there tomorrow."

"Your mother didn't take such notions out of your head," she reminded him heatedly. "Why must you oppose what I want to do, when it's exactly what you wanted to do when you were young?"

Her father stopped his stalking and waved the letter at her again. "I had a vocation. I was born for the stage. You are a silly little girl with a moon-struck notion that you will have to get over. Go and pack your things. I am through discussing this."

He turned his back with an air of finality, and she knew further argument would be useless. Nevertheless, she paused at the door.

"Do you know what I think?" she asked. "I think you're still afraid of your mother." And out she went, leaving that parting shot behind her.

He closed the door none too gently, and Lauré knew that she had hit home. Angrily she turned toward her own room, then paused again in surprise. Across the hall, leaning in his doorway, stood Cole Drummond.

"What was all that ruckus about?" he asked. "I'll bet they could hear you shouting at each other about good manners clear to Canal Street. It's a good thing Mother and Jessamyn are out."

It made everything that much worse to have Cole pick on her at this moment. Why couldn't he pay attention to her when she was looking and acting her best? Now she was ready to include him in her own fury, whether she loved him or not. But she had no more than opened her mouth to tell him what she thought of his eavesdropping, when he caught her by the wrist and drew her toward the stairs.

"Come along and tell me all about it," he said.

His grip on her wrist gave her no choice, and she allowed herself to be led downstairs and out into the shadows of the summerhouse. An azalea bush flowered nearby, pink blossoms shining amidst green foliage.

"There," Cole said, lowering her to a bench, "you're calming down a bit. It's always harder to stay angry when you're in a garden. I really didn't hear the whole thing—just your voices. I opened my door when I heard you come into the hall. What's happened?"

She was still breathing fast, and she had to take a quick gulp of air before she could speak. "My grandmother has ordered my father to send me to her house in the Vieux

Carré for what she calls an 'extended visit'—so she can teach me how to be a lady. And Father says I'm to go."

Cole's eyes were kind, and that unnerved her further. Her anger vanished and she began to sniff and blink her lashes rapidly.

He smiled at her. "If I were a gentleman from one of Jessamyn's novels, I'd have a snowy handkerchief to offer you. But I don't have a spare at the moment, so you'd better not cry. Anyway, I don't see anything so awful about going to visit your grandmother."

"How would you like to go and live with someone who didn't approve of anything about you and only wanted to make every inch of you over?" she demanded. "It will be horrible!"

"Oh, I don't know," he said. "Maybe you're lucky." He plucked a sprig of azalea and studied its bright beauty for a moment before he bent to thrust it into her blond hair. She held very still at his touch, wanting to cry again.

"Lucky?" she echoed.

"I wish she'd ask me to visit her. I don't know of anyone in New Orleans I'd like to know better. Think of all the exciting history she's lived through. She is a true *grande dame,* and she belongs to a time that's nearly gone. I don't think much of it will weather over into the new century— there are too many big changes afoot."

Lauré gaped in surprise, and he went on.

"Antoinette Beaudine was a young girl at the time when New Orleans really belonged to the Creoles. They must have been a wonderful people in their prime. They could laugh and cry and be practical and foolish, all in the same breath. They knew how to feel, and how to live. During the war they were as brave as any people in the South. Madame Beaudine has lived through all that, Lauré. Through the occupation of New Orleans by Northern soldiers, through terrible yellow-fever epidemics. What do you care if she tries to teach you her ideas about good manners, when she has all that besides to give you? There's nothing wrong, after all, with holding to high standards, even if other people grow lax. I admire her for it."

The anger had seeped out of Lauré, and with it all the prickly, childish resentment. *I know why I love him,* she thought. *It's because he is so very much worth loving.*

"You'll make a fine teacher," she said softly.

There was another reason why she did not want to go away. If she went to her grandmother's, there would be no opportunity to see Cole. And if she could not see him, how was she ever to get him to see her? *really* see her? How could she bear to be banished?

He chuckled. "You mean I'll be good at persuading people to do what they don't want to do? I suppose that's part of a teacher's job, at that."

She answered him seriously. "I think you'll understand the children in your classes and you'll make them want to think for themselves. You'll like them and they'll feel that and like you back." She held out her hand to him. "Maybe I'm your first pupil. All right—I'll go to my grandmother's, and I'll try to get something out of the visit."

He pulled her up from the bench and she almost went into his arms, but he stepped back in time to avoid the contact. The movement was deliberate, and she winced, knowing it.

"Maybe you'll need to portray a woman like your grandmother on the stage someday," he said dryly. "You can get that out of it too."

She nodded as they walked back to the house. A broken heart, she had heard, made one a better actress, and undoubtedly she would end up with a very broken heart.

"There's another thing," Cole said just before he left her at the stairway. "It may be that your grandmother wants something from you too."

Lauré shook her head. She could not imagine that. All her grandmother wanted was a lump of clay she could model into a pattern she approved. And a lump of clay Lauré Beaudine would not, could not, be. Back in her room she took the sprig of azalea from her hair and looked at it thoughtfully.

By the next afternoon, when Celeste Drummond was ready to drive her to the French Quarter, Lauré had resigned herself to endure the visit to her grandmother, while holding to an inner resistance. She half hoped that Cole might come with them for the drive, but he disappeared in the morning without even saying good-by.

At the Beaudine house, Arcadie came to welcome her and invited Mrs. Drummond in for coffee. Celeste, however, graciously declined on the score of errands to do, and Lauré went upstairs with her cousin. Arcadie slipped an affectionate arm about her waist and whispered to her as they reached the second-floor gallery.

"It will be marvelous to have a cousin my own age in the house. I do hope we can keep it from being too dull for you. Tante Sophie and Tante Gaby have gone across the lake for a long visit, so the house is very quiet."

"It won't be dull with you here," Lauré assured her. It was not this gay little cousin whose company she dreaded.

"Where is my grandmother?"

"At the moment," Arcadie said, "she is in Grand-père's study discussing certain business papers with—with Marcel Duval." Arcadie broke off, a faint color sweeping her face, her eyes the picture of entreaty. Hesitantly, she spoke again. "Cousin, will you do something for me?"

"Of course," Lauré said, though she felt uneasy at the mention of Marcel's name.

Arcadie went on in a little rush. "In a moment Grand-mère will dismiss him. When he comes out, I will take you at once to the door. Then perhaps you can keep Grand-mère occupied while I have a few moments with Marcel. The way I am chaperoned, I can never have a second alone with him."

"I'll do my best—" Lauré began, but at that moment the study door at the end of the hallway opened and Marcel stepped out, bowing respectfully to Madame Beaudine. Then he saw Lauré and exclaimed out loud.

"Mam'selle Lauré! How fine to see you again. I understand that you are to visit in this house for a time. I hope I shall have the privilege—"

Grand-mère cut in on his speech a little brusquely. "You will have the privilege of hurrying those papers back to your father, young man. Good afternoon, Lauré. Arcadie, please take your cousin to her room so that she may settle herself. Then you may bring her to me here."

Grand-mère vanished into her study, but her commands rang in the air. Marcel bowed regretfully over Lauré's hand and took himself off with no more than a casual smile for Arcadie. The little cousin was sober as she led the way to Lauré's room.

14. Two Letters

FEELING uncomfortable, Lauré followed her cousin along a second-floor gallery to a room overlooking the courtyard below. She wished Marcel wouldn't behave in such a foolish way. Her mind had been so intent on other matters that she had forgotten that the Duvals lived next door and that she would be sure to meet Marcel in this house. She had done her best to avoid him ever since the ball, and she knew now that she was less interested in him than ever. So why must he look at her in a moon-struck way which Arcadie must surely have noticed?

Her cousin pushed open a door and motioned Lauré to enter. "I hope you'll be comfortable here," she said courteously, but now there was a reserve in her tone that had not been present before.

To Lauré's eyes the room was a delight. It won her in spite of any resistance she might have harbored. Here only lovely old-fashioned furniture had been used. There was a huge four-poster bed with a blue half tester above. A great *armoire*—the wardrobe closet of the Creoles—opened to receive the few dresses she had brought with her. A delicately carved dressing table of rosewood stood near a window, with a small seat before it. On the marble slab of the washstand was a china basin, the inside of the bowl sprinkled with painted rosebuds, and there was a graceful china pitcher to match.

"It's a perfect room," Lauré said.

"You are pleased? For a little while it was my mother's room, long ago when she visited this house as a girl—

before she married my father," Arcadie said. "Across the courtyard is the room that belonged to your father. Grand-mère has never changed its furnishings. She does not allow it to be used."

Tactfully, Arcadie moved to the door, to leave her cousin alone. But just before she closed it, she turned back to Lauré, once more flushing deeply.

"Tell me, Cousin—was it Marcel who sent you the call-out for the Carnival ball?"

For just a moment Lauré thought of pleading that her partner had been masked, that she could not be sure. But she did not want to be dishonest with Arcadie, even to save her feelings.

"Yes, it was Marcel," she confessed. "But believe me, there will be no more invitations that I will accept. I have no wish—"

"Please—it does not matter," Arcadie said with dignity. "If you will excuse me—Grand-mère is calling." And she hurried off before Lauré could say anything more.

Lauré's portmanteau had been brought to the room, and she opened it to take out the box with the cameo necklace. Her first duty must be to return the necklace to her grand-mother. At the same time she unpacked the picture of her mother and set it against the dressing table mirror. She did not want to forget that New Orleans—in particular, her grandmother—had rejected Mary Beaudine. In a side pocket of the portmanteau she found the little Juliet cap she had tucked into it in New York. But that she left where it was, wondering when, if ever, she would need it.

Then she went to the window and stood looking down at the shadows of late afternoon deepening in the courtyard.

The scent of flowers came to her sweetly, and a strange nostalgia seemed to flow through her. A nostalgia for something she had never known. It was as if she might at last find her roots in this place, as if all the years of the past before she was born might now belong to her as they had never belonged before.

This room had been occupied by those related to her, even though she had never known them. Across the courtyard was the room in which her father had spent his boyhood years. He had walked these very galleries, had perhaps dipped his fingers into the fountain below and dreamed there of the future. This feeling was what she had wanted of this house the first time she had glimpsed it, but until now the feeling had been withheld from her. Madame Beaudine might be a stranger to her, Arcadie might withdraw—but the house itself had spoken to her.

She must find a way to make Arcadie understand how she felt about Marcel, and to make Marcel understand too. But for the moment she could not think of these matters. She could not even hold to a sense of resentment because of the way New Orleans had treated her mother.

It was in this bemused state that she went with Arcadie to see her grandmother. The old lady sat at a high-back *éscritoire,* writing with a quill pen. She thrust its point into a brass container of shot and set her letter aside as Lauré came in. Arcadie left her cousin at the door and went away.

"Sit down, if you please," said Grand-mère 'Toinette.

Lauré took a chair opposite her, sitting upright on its edge, the box with the necklace in her hands.

"This was your grandfather's study," the old lady

informed her. "These are his books and possessions, and I have left them exactly as he liked to see them."

"Just as you have left my father's room as it used to be," Lauré said, her thoughts still upon this house where her father had lived as a boy.

Madame Beaudine said nothing, and Lauré glanced about her grandfather's study. The carpet was a faded wine color, and so were the draperies at the long shuttered doors which opened upon the gallery overlooking the street. It was a dim, cool room, a room for work and quiet thinking. Relaxing a little, Lauré leaned back in her chair.

"The first thing a Creole girl must learn," Grand-mère said, "is to sit up straight on all occasions. The back of a chair is for decoration. It is not to be leaned against."

Lauré sat up as if she had been pricked and held out the box to her grandmother. "Thank you for lending me the necklace. I was very proud to wear it at the ball."

Madame Beaudine took the box and opened it, her lips curving into softer lines. "I am glad it gave you pleasure, my child. Perhaps one day I shall leave it to you in my will. If you please me while you are here, that is. Please me by learning quickly."

Lauré knew that she must make her position clear at once. She had come here reluctantly, and while she was here she must not pretend what would never be true. Even though her grandmother frightened her a little, she must speak out.

"I'm afraid I will never please you," she said. "Not because I won't try, but because I mean to follow my father and go on the stage."

"Ah, yes," said her grandmother, sounding unexpectedly mild, "so you have told me. And why, may I ask, do you have this unsuitable ambition?"

Lauré thought about that for a moment. "I'm not sure exactly. It's just that I've always felt this way. I've always dreamed of the day when I would be with my father again, as I was when I was small."

How could she put into words the feeling she had about the magic of backstage—the longing to know again the warmth and gaiety and friendliness that had existed there to enfold a little girl in safe, loving arms. To regain all that she must be a good enough actress for her father to reckon with. She had been working toward that goal for as long as she could remember. Now, faltering a little, she tried to put some of these things into words.

Her grandmother listened to her attentively and, surprisingly enough, she did not dismiss Lauré's words as her father always dismissed them. When Lauré broke off in embarrassment because she could no longer struggle to make something so tenuous sound reasonable, Madame Beaudine rose and walked to a bookshelf. From among other volumes she selected one and handed it to Lauré.

"Let me hear you read," she commanded. "Open the pages at random and read whatever you find."

Once more Lauré held in her hands a volume of Shakespeare's plays. Somewhat astonished, she riffled the pages and they fell open to *The Merchant of Venice*. Lauré had no need to read the words of Portia's famous "quality of mercy" speech. She raised her head and spoke the words as she had done so many times before her own mirror back in New York. But it was very different speaking them here before this Creole grandmother.

Grand-mère 'Toinette listened without expression as

Lauré finished the speech and went on with the scene. Then she lifted her hand in a signal to stop.

"This is what you consider acting?" she asked.

"I'm not a professional," Lauré defended herself. "I have had to learn alone."

Her grandmother shook her head frankly. "You would not, I think, pass a fair test in our New Orleans amateur theatricals, of which we are so fond. Besides, you have given me all the wrong reasons for becoming an actress. There is only one reason I could truly understand—the one that was your father's, but that reason you have not given me."

Lauré stiffened with indignation, but she did not lower her gaze. "Just the same," she said, "I mean to be an actress someday. Nothing is going to stop me."

"We shall see," Grand-mère said calmly. "In the meantime, let us get on with your training as a Creole housewife. Perhaps you will marry a Creole man in good time and give up this foolishness about the stage." The old lady seemed to recall something and she gave Lauré a penetrating look. "Did I notice a special interest in you on the part of Marcel Duval?"

Lauré was startled. Her grandmother missed nothing. "I—I hope not," she faltered.

"And why do you hope not? He would make a most suitable husband for a young lady of good family."

"I have no interest in him," Lauré admitted. "He seems a pleasant young man, but I'd only want him for a friend."

"A young girl has little wisdom about such matters," Grand-mère said. "What one feels before marriage is of no consequence. True affection grows afterward. Do you think I felt for my husband before marriage what I came to feel for him later?"

This was not something Lauré could argue with her grandmother. Age held the winning cards of experience, against which youth could bring no arguments, but only a strong instinct.

"Besides," Lauré said, "there is Arcadie. Her heart is set on Marcel. I would never want to hurt her." Grand-mère's deep-set eyes brightened and she nodded her approval. "Your feeling is to your credit, my child. Arcadie's sentiments have been made all too clear. In this case they may be quite suitable. You will forgive my questions—I wished to know more of your character."

"But if—if Marcel doesn't care for Arcadie as she cares for him—"

"That is a matter of no importance," Grand-mère said. "It is natural for young men to have passing fancies. Next year, when 'Cadie is of age, M'sieur Robert Duval and I will make arrangements for the marriage of his son to my grand-daughter. The children will be guided by our wishes. It is fortunate that 'Cadie feels as she does—though not necessary. They are suited to each other—love, as I say, will follow in marriage."

Arcadie tapped on the door just then, and Grand-mère called to her to enter. She brought a letter for her grandmother, and Madame Beaudine invited her to stay.

"We have been speaking of love," she said, smiling fondly at Arcadie. "Of love and marriage. I can well remember my own foolish youth when I once fancied myself in love, though in truth I knew nothing of the real sentiment."

"Was that the time when a duel was fought over you,

Grandmother?" Lauré asked.

The old lady frowned, and Arcadie gasped at so bold a question.

"A lady," Grand-mère said with dignity, "knows nothing of such matters. She keeps herself free of all *scandale*."

Lauré smiled, somehow less afraid of her grandmother now. "Underneath every lady there's a girl," she said. "It must have been very exciting, even if you had to pretend you didn't know anything about it."

"You think it is exciting to have two young men trying to kill themselves in so wasteful a way?" her grandmother asked dryly.

"I didn't say it was right," Lauré protested, "or that I'd approve of it. I only said it must have been exciting. I hope no one was hurt."

Again her grandmother's eyes rested upon Lauré in a long look of mingled astonishment and disapproval. "In my day the young did not question their elders about matters which should not be discussed."

"Do you mean that you've never been able to talk about something like that? Not even to girls your own age when it happened? How could you hold it back all these years? Were you in love with one of the men?"

Grand-mère flung up her hands in a gesture of despair, but Lauré saw the faint smile that had curved her straight, firm mouth.

"You ask questions like a small child. My *maman* said I would be the death of her—fancying myself in love when I knew nothing at all about the true emotion. Yes—I thought myself in love with one of the two."

This time Arcadie forgot herself and asked an eager question. "What was he like? Do tell us, Grand-mère."

"What was he like?" The old lady echoed the words doubtfully and then shook her head. "*Hélas!* I cannot remember. Even his name escapes me, though he was the one who wounded his opponent, winning the duel."

Lauré listened in astonishment. Her grandmother had been in love with a young man who had fought a duel for her sake—and now she could not even remember his name. Somehow this was a chilling thought. Would the time come someday when Lauré Beaudine would not be able to remember the name of Cole Drummond?

"Perhaps I forgot him because it was his opponent whom I married," Grand-mère said. "Claude Beaudine was the young man he wounded. Later my parents arranged a marriage between us—though that had nothing to do with the duel. Perhaps there was even a time when I rebelled against the arrangement. Though only inwardly, of course. My elders knew best and never for a moment have I regretted marrying my husband."

She sighed, her thoughts clearly upon the more recent past, of which Claude Beaudine had been so important a part. Then she roused herself, asking her granddaughters to excuse her while she read the letter Arcadie had brought.

While Grand-mère opened the envelope, Lauré carried the book of plays back to its place on the shelf and let her eye wander over other titles. Her grandmother's little cry of distress made her turn quickly from the shelves.

Grand-mère had risen and carried the letter to the gallery door where she could have better light. There was a furrow between her brows as she read it through. When she had finished she looked sadly at Arcadie.

"Duprés has found a buyer for Les Ombres. The place will go out of my hands shortly. A man from the North."

"But this is what you wish, is it not, Grand-mère?" Arcadie asked.

"It is what I must do," the old lady said. "I can no longer deal with the burden of a plantation house." She stood by the window, silent and a little sad, and Arcadie explained softly to Lauré.

"Our great-great-grandparents on the Fortier side built the house and once owned a great sugar plantation across the Mississippi. 'Les Ombres,' they called it—The Shadows. Such a beautiful place! Grand-mère is of course sad to see it leave her hands. When I was small she used to take me there to stay sometimes. But now most of the land around it has been sold, and no one lives on the grounds except the caretaker and his wife."

Grand-mère folded the letter precisely and returned it to its envelope. Then she turned to Lauré, seeming to make up her mind about something.

"Before long I shall go there for the last time," she said. "You and Arcadie shall come with me. It is fitting, Lauré, that you see this other home of your ancestors. And I, of course, must bid it adieu. If you will excuse me, children, I will write my answer immediately."

She returned to the *escritoire,* and the two girls went quietly from the room.

"It will be sad to see the place again," Arcadie said, "now that it is going out of the family. How fine it must have been in the old days, when Grand-mère was young and there were so many balls, such gaiety."

But Lauré was hardly listening to her cousin's words.

166

There was something she wanted to make clear without further delay, and before any greater misunderstanding could grow on Arcadie's part. She stood beside her cousin at the iron railing overlooking the sunny court.

"I've told no one else," she whispered to Arcadie. "But I would like to tell you. I think perhaps I am in love." She saw alarm leap into Arcadie's eyes and she hurried on. "I think I am in love with Cole Drummond. You won't tell anyone, will you?"

The alarm faded as Arcadie's small face lighted with pleasure. She put her arms quickly about her cousin and gave her a warm squeeze.

"But that is marvelous! And what a suitable marriage it will make, Cousin. Now you will forget about the stage and settle down to be a good wife right here in New Orleans. You will be—"

"Marriage!" Lauré cried. "He doesn't even know I'm alive. And of course I am going on the stage. I have no intention of staying in New Orleans."

Clearly Lauré's outburst made not the slightest impression on her cousin. Arcadie reached into a pocket of her dress and brought out a second envelope.

"I did not wish to give you this before Grand-mère," she said smiling shyly. "It is a letter for you from Cole Drummond himself. It arrived by messenger only a little while ago. So you see—he does indeed know that you are alive."

15. Les Ombres

Lauré took the letter to her room and sat down before the little rosewood dressing table to open it. She found that her fingers were clumsy with haste as she slit the envelope. Had her grandmother once felt this way about the young man whose name she had forgotten? Oh, surely not!

Cole's handwriting was clear and bold—the writing of someone who knew his own mind. Lauré read eagerly at first, then with growing despair.

Dear Lauré,

I knew I would be gone this morning before you were up, but I did not want to say good-by to you last night. I dislike good-bys intensely, and I knew this one would be so very final.

I am going back to the country to work out details concerning the school where I am to teach in the fall. This time I believe I will stay for a while and become acquainted with some of my pupils and their parents. I am happier there than I am here in New Orleans, where I must for the time being live in an atmosphere of disapproval. It will be best for my parents too if they understand that I do not mean to change my mind. Perhaps someday they will forgive me for what I am doing.

All this is about myself—and I had meant to write about you. I hope you haven't minded my teasing you sometimes, Lauré. Perhaps I am not the sort to play the role of a gallant to the extent that pleases a girl. But I like your spirit and I admire your determination to do the thing that you think most important, just as I must take the course that calls to me. If that is what you truly want, let nothing stop you. Perhaps someday a Louisiana schoolteacher will sit in an audience and applaud you on the stage. And I will tell my pupils that long ago I knew the famous Lauré Beaudine as a young girl.

But don't miscast yourself, Lauré. You have spirit, yes, but you are a white rose too—never a shrew like Kate. When you become an actress, find the roles that suit you. Don't be scornful of Juliet.

May good fortune bless you.

Faithfully yours,

Cole Drummond

Lauré's lashes were wet with tears as she finished reading. How could she bear it never to see him again? Yet she knew that to continue to see him, if she returned to the Drummonds, would mean only a later, still more painful parting. Since their roads had to separate, it was better that they divide at once, so that the loss might make a clean, sharp wound, from which she could begin to recover.

Now the wound had been made. It ached whichever way she turned, and there was no ease to be found anywhere.

She folded the letter carefully and put it away. It was something she would keep all her life—though she would never need it to remind her of Cole Drummond's name.

After a while, when her eyes were dry and she could trust herself, she went downstairs to join Arcadie in the court-yard. Her cousin stood beside a huge clay jar, stirring water in it with a stick. She looked around quickly at Lauré, her eyes clearly questioning. But when she saw Lauré's face, she understood that all was not well and returned her atten-tion to the task before her.

"What are you doing?" Lauré asked, forcing herself to sound matter-of-fact.

"This is something I learned to do when I was a little

girl," Arcadie said, not looking at her. "When water is brought from the river for household use, it is muddy and impure. So we drop a lump of alum into it and stir for a long while. When the mud settles in the bottom of the olla, the water is left clear and fit to use."

"Let me stir for a while," Lauré said.

Arcadie gave her the stick and Lauré stirred the water round and round in the big jar until it spun of its own force, turning about the stick, just as life seemed to spin on about Lauré, while she made only the most automatic of responses.

At eighteen, however, it is not possible to remain an automaton forever. Lauré was no stick to permit life to spin about her while she took no part in it. As Shakespeare himself had written, one did not die of love. The life of New Orleans in spring was not something Lauré could remain indifferent to: not when all her senses responded to it with a hunger for beauty that she could satisfy only by her awareness of living.

How rich the pageant of flowers! Pink camellias and brilliant azaleas, roses by the thousand, scenting the air so sweetly that one almost forgot the open gutters of the Vieux Carré. At night, when Lauré lay beneath a lace-trimmed Creole mosquito netting she could hear a mockingbird in the courtyard, singing its heart out to the moon. She closed her eyes, listening, aching a little with the beauty of the sound. When the oleanders ceased to bloom, Arcadie said, the mockingbird would cease to sing and be silent all summer long. If only her heart could cease its aching as easily.

Perhaps being in love, even when it was so sad an emotion, made her all the more sensitive to the throbbing life that crowded the world all about her. True, there was always an inner loneliness, a longing for him to be there to share each small, lovely experience, but perhaps she was the richer because even to love without being loved in return was at least living.

Now she grew accustomed to the excitement and bustle of everyday life in the French Quarter. In the early morning, before the heat of the day had commenced, she liked to sit on the gallery overlooking Royal Street and watch the colorful pageant below. Royal Street didn't need Carnival time to make it dance with color and life.

There was always the traffic of drays pulled by mules, of carriages and spirited horses, the shouts of drivers, the rattle of harness. On the sidewalks vendors called their varied wares, each with his own special song or cry: the berry woman, the coal peddler, the amazing chimney sweep with his high top hat and wailing call. Negro women went by in guinea blue, huge baskets of laundry balanced expertly on their chignoned heads. Drinking in all this life and color, Lauré took it hungrily to her heart and made it a part of her own experience and memory, so that it would never leave her.

Of course there were many duties about the house to keep her busy. Grand-mère did not believe in idle hands. Lauré helped Arcadie wash by hand every crystal tear-drop in all the chandeliers, drying and polishing them to a new luster, then returning each to its proper place. She learned the secret of making delicious crawfish bisque, and to cook rice to pearly fluffiness.

No word came from her father, and that left her with an uneasy, uncertain feeling. For all she knew, he might suddenly decide to leave New Orleans and go off without her. She had been able to do nothing about his request to help him make his peace with his mother. Grand-mère still refused to have the topic of Jules Beaudine brought up for discussion. No further word, of course, came from Cole Drummond.

One thing Lauré managed to do. On an afternoon when she knew that Marcel Duval had come to see her grandmother, she went to her room and got the gold and coral pin he had given her as a Carnival favor. She hovered on the gallery until she heard his step in the hall, and then she went to meet him.

At once the ardent light came into his eyes, but this time she did not let it trouble her. She had begun to suspect that Marcel could turn that light off and on as easily as one did a lamp.

"I want to give back your pin," she told him directly. "You shouldn't have given me so fine a gift at Carnival." Marcel was a dramatic young man. He smote his forehead with one hand in exaggerated despair. "But this is unheard of, Mam'selle Lauré! It is not proper to return a Carnival favor. I have only to deny that it was I who gave it to you. After all, you danced with one who was masked. This can only mean that you detest me."

"Don't be ridiculous," she said, holding out the pin. "I like you very much, but I really can't accept this as a gift."

She could have chosen no better way to offend him. His look went suddenly chill.

"You will do me the favor to keep it," he said. "I understand that you will someday act with your father on the stage. Perhaps you will wear it in some great role and remember New Orleans."

He made her a stiff little bow and strode away, the picture of insulted masculinity. Lauré smiled to herself, watching him go. She could not believe that she had wounded him very deeply. The coral pin pricked her palm as she closed her fingers about it. She did not need this token to remind her of New Orleans—not when she had a small gilt shoe tossed from a float. But perhaps she would wear the pin to fasten the mantle of a stage costume someday. And then she would sigh—wondering what could have been the name of that young man with whom she had danced. . . .

It was a few days later that Madame Beaudine sent her cook and maid ahead to the plantation. This trip had been postponed long enough, and soon there would be no more opportunity. Lauré and Arcadie must pack a few things and make ready to leave tomorrow. The drive would be a fairly long one.

It began the next day with a trip by ferry across the roiling yellow Mississippi. Then for some distance they followed a winding bayou, overhung by ancient trees. Now and then a small boat would drift by along the waterway, and sometimes Lauré would glimpse a wide-eyed child staring back at them.

As they followed the dusty country road, Grand-mère spoke of her own childhood and life on the plantation.

"My grandfather, Auguste Fortier, came here from the West Indies after a slave uprising," she said. "He built his house for hot weather in the West Indian manner, yet with touches of Louisiana too. All this sugar-cane land we are driving through once belonged to the Fortiers. Now, soon, none of it will belong to us."

She fell sadly into silence and did not speak again until the carriage turned up the driveway to the house. The drive wound beneath live oak trees, their branches arching overhead and dripping long gray strands of Spanish moss. No longer was the driveway kept free of weeds, and tropical vegetation crowded close about.

Only near the house had a space been kept clear, so that there was still a sense of spacious lawns in front of the building. Lauré saw it first across these lawns—a house built for comfort as well as beauty. It was of cypress wood and brick, its first story set high off the ground, with a double flight of steps leading up to the entrance. The brick had been stuccoed over like the houses of the Vieux Carré and painted a yellow that had weathered in the sun to a warm peach color.

Long columns marched across the front from ground to roof, and behind the railing that joined them a deep gallery sheltered the interior of the house from the sun. The steeply pitched roof was of cypress, with several dormer windows cutting into it.

Grand-mère shook her head over what she saw as she left the carriage. "It will be better for the house when this man from the North takes it over and makes the needed repairs. Though I had never thought to see a Yankee living within these walls."

The girls followed her quietly up the steps and across the wide gallery behind the pillars. In the stillness Lauré thought of the gay voices that must once have sounded here. She could almost hear the echo of laughter drifting down through the years.

After the warm sunlight outside, the high-ceilinged

rooms and hallways were dim and cool. A great parlor opened on the right, its furniture shrouded in white dust covers. From elaborately carved plaster medallions on the ceiling hung dusty chandeliers, which must once have known the light of a hundred candles.

A graceful stairway curved upward at the rear of the hall, and again Grand-mère led the way, the girls following. Upstairs three bedrooms had been prepared for occupancy—the large one for Madame Beaudine, two smaller adjoining rooms for Lauré and Arcadie.

The caretaker and his wife welcomed them, and Grand-mère spoke with the two for a little while before she removed her bonnet and set about bathing her face and hands in the cool water provided.

Lauré found that a side dormer cut into her room, and because of the close thickness of trees outside the window and the faded green of the wallpaper the room had a lovely undersea glow to it. Arcadie looked in from the next room and exclaimed over the restful green dusk.

When the girls had refreshed themselves, they rejoined Madame Beaudine, to find her lying upon a chaise longue with cushions piled behind her.

"All this is part of a life that is over," she murmured sadly, looking about her. "Lauré, bring that hassock near. I wish to speak with you."

"You will excuse me, Grand-mère?" Arcadie said tactfully. "I'd like to go outside and visit some of the places I knew as a child."

Her grandmother nodded, and Lauré brought the hassock near the chaise longue and sat down upon it. She had no idea what was coming. At the house in the Vieux Carré life had not been as dull as she had feared—her grandmother had always kept her busy. But there had been little real conversation between them. Now something of portent seemed to be in the air.

"So many memories cling to these rooms," Grand-mère said softly. "When I come here my girlhood does not seem so far away. Or my early days as a bride. I met my husband for the first time under this very roof. I fear I was unkind to him in the beginning. But he was never a man to change his mind, once it was made up. When he decided that I was the girl he would marry, I stood no chance of escaping, even if I had so wished."

"But I thought the marriage was arranged by your parents," Lauré said.

"Of course. But at his insistence. There were no objections, since it was highly suitable."

"He never changed his mind about my father, either?" Lauré asked.

Grand-mère had rested the gold-headed cane against the arm of her chair and she raised both blue-veined hands to smooth back the gray hair at her temples. Her fingers rested there lightly at Lauré's words, and the old lady's eyes searched her granddaughter's with penetration.

"That is true," she agreed at length.

"But you are different," Lauré said gently. "There isn't any reason why you shouldn't change your mind. At least there is no longer any reason."

Slowly Grand-mère's hands came down, folded themselves gracefully in her lap.

"This is one of the things of which I wish to speak with you, my child. I can think more freely here, where I do not feel M'sieur, my husband, watching me from his portrait. Tell me—how would your father feel about seeing his mother again? Is he angry, resentful?"

Lauré shook her head. "When you first invited me to come to see you, he asked me to help him make his peace with you. This is the main reason why he has come to New Orleans. But I think he is still a little boy where you are concerned and still a little afraid. He won't come unless you call him, Grandmother."

"Then I shall call," Madame Beaudine said decisively. "I shall wait no longer. But it is of you, also, that I wish to speak, Lauré. There is this matter of your going on the stage—"

Lauré sat up straight on the hassock, waiting as her grandmother paused. After a moment of silence the old lady went on.

"Tell me this, Lauré. If your father should continue to set himself against this desire of yours—what then?"

This was something Lauré had always refused to consider. All her plans and hopes were bound up in going upon the stage in her father's company, under his wing.

That was the only way she ever thought of the future.

"I'm not sure I know what you mean," she said.

"Would you go on by yourself? If your father refused to help you, would you face the difficulties, make your own way alone? That is what I mean."

"Why—I suppose so," Lauré said. But she had never truly faced this possibility. It was a frightening one, now that her grandmother placed it squarely before her. "Anyway, I needn't make that choice," she hurried to add. "I'm sure Father will want to help me, once he sees that I'm in earnest."

"And that you have talent?" Grand-mère suggested.

"Of course," Lauré said. "I know you didn't think much of my reading, but I can do better than that. The circumstances weren't right when I read to you—it was not a fair test. But so far my father has never given me a chance. He refuses to listen to me so much as read a scene from a play."

"I see," her grandmother said. "Well—perhaps it is up to us to change all that."

Lauré stared at her. "What do you mean, Grandmother?"

"It is possible that I have a plan," the old lady said. "But I must think about it more carefully. I am not yet ready to tell you."

And so the matter was left, though Lauré felt curious and tantalized. Her grandmother, as she was coming to realize, was a woman of imagination and invention. There was no telling what she might have up her sleeve. It was hard to believe that she might come over to her granddaughter's side in this matter. Whatever this plan might be, Lauré did not altogether trust her grandmother's purpose.

She went outside to find Arcadie, and they walked together about the immediate grounds of the house. The shadows of afternoon were lengthening, so that the shape of the house lay across the waters of the little bayou that wound beside it. One understood how the place had come by its name. Around at the back were small brick buildings, almost hidden now by undergrowth. These, Arcadie said, had once been the slave quarters. A queer little six-sided structure of whitewashed brick, with a steeply pointed roof, had been the *garçonnière*—a house for the bachelors of the family and their friends. It was the Creole custom to provide separate quarters for them in this manner.

A sense of melancholy haunted Lauré as she walked the grounds with her cousin. What a loss it seemed that this house must go out of the family, that it could no longer be kept up in the manner of former days. Arcadie agreed that this was sad—but what could one do? Without doubt, it was too great a burden for Grand-mère to carry any longer. All over the plantation area in Louisiana, these beautiful old houses were falling into disuse. Perhaps there would come a time when they would exist no longer, unless something was done to save them.

Supper that night was a strange meal, served in a vast dining room that was many steps away from the kitchen. As they sat at one end of a long table, Lauré felt that she and her grandmother and cousin were dwarfed by the expanse of a room built for a large family and many visitors. Afterward, when the moon was up, the three women strolled upon the shadowy lawn and looked up at the great, luminous house, silvery white beneath the moon.

That night, as Lauré lay wakeful in her bed, she sensed the murmur of sounds that were not the sounds of New Orleans. There was a wind sighing in the forest all about, and the hum of insects on a warm night, the cry of some small animal, perhaps in pain.

Where was Cole tonight? she wondered. When Arcadie sighed softly in the next room, Lauré slipped out of bed and went through the open door to sit on the edge of her cousin's bed.

"What lies west of us?" she asked. "More plantations?"

"Not around here," Arcadie said. "The plantations always clung to the river and the bayous nearby. West of us lies the country where Cole Drummond wants to teach."

Lauré stared at her cousin in the shadow-filled moonlight. "Do you mean that Cole might be somewhere near us now?"

"It is possible," Arcadie said. "But he might as well be many miles away, for all that you are likely to see him."

"Yes, I know," Lauré said, and went back to her own bed. Nevertheless, it was comforting to think Cole might be not too many miles away—even though she could not see him.

16. *The Plans of Madame Beaudine*

THE next morning Grand-mère announced that since she would never in her life come to this house again, they might as well stay for a while longer. After all, now that she had seen the house, she realized how much must be done to put it in order for the new owner.

Not a dusty corner must remain; not a cobweb. Every chandelier crystal—Arcadie groaned—must sparkle. Never must it be said that a Fortier left her home in anything but immaculate order. *Allons!* they had work to do.

In the days that followed, Lauré discovered just how hard a Creole lady could work when the stake was a shining house and she had little hired help for a place so huge. Not even Aunt Judith in her periodic house-cleaning attacks was more industrious than Antoinette Fortier Beaudine. Arcadie complained of broken nails, and Lauré of cricks in her neck and bruised knees, but Grand-mère was both commander and private in their war upon grime, and there were times when she seemed the youngest of the three.

"Youth is soft today!" she repeated scornfully at intervals.

"When I was your age . . ."

There was another matter, too, that occupied Grand-mère—her plans concerning Jules Beaudine. Lauré knew that she had written her son a letter, but neither Lauré nor Arcadie was told its contents.

By the time an answer came, the magnolias were blooming and the grounds about the house were glorious with waxy white blossoms. When her son's letter arrived, Grand mère bore it away to her room to read it alone, and she did not come out for some little while. When at last she called Lauré and Arcadie to come to her, Lauré saw that she had been weeping. But she did not look unhappy.

"He is coming, *mes enfants!*" she cried. "My son is coming to visit us at Les Ombres!"

Arcadie murmured that this was indeed wonderful, but Lauré was too moved to speak at all. This, she knew, was what her father had longed for, and clearly his mother longed for it too. How satisfying then that the meeting would take place here, where the shadow of Jules Beaudine's father would not fall as sternly as it would in the Vieux Carré!

Grand-mère's bright eyes were alive with plans. "*Ça va sans dire*—it goes without saying—that we must hurry with our arrangements for the little performance you will give, Lauré, my dear."

"Performance?" Lauré repeated blankly. "I?"

Grand-mère thumped her cane on the floor for emphasis. "*Mais, certainement!* Surely you wish to perform for your father, do you not? To prove to him the soundness of your ambition? Then we must plan, rehearse."

"But—but I don't see—" Suddenly Lauré was frightened.

It was as if the strong current of the Mississippi had caught her up and was sweeping her along helplessly to disaster. Truly, her grandmother was just such a current.

"Stop stammering and use your very good head, my dear," Grand-mère said. "I have brought with me a play for this very purpose, and I have chosen a scene that will show off your talents nicely. Your father, naturally, will wish to please me, and he will not refuse when I tell him he is to witness this little performance. He is to witness and judge for himself. I have even brought with me some possible costume materials."

Grand-mère went to her dresser and took a small flat volume from a drawer. She held it out to Lauré, who saw that it was a copy of *Romeo and Juliet*.

"Take it, take it!" Grand-mère commanded, as Lauré hesitated. "Please examine the scene I have chosen and see if it meets with your approval."

Lauré took the book as if she were half afraid of it and let her eyes stray down the page. The scene Grand-mère had marked was in the second act, where Juliet has sent her nurse with a message to Romeo and now awaits her return.

"Read, then, if you please," Grand-mère requested. "Let me hear how it sounds on your lips."

There was nothing to do but obey, and Lauré read aloud stiffly:

" 'The clock struck nine when I did send the nurse,
In half an hour she promised to return.
Perchance she cannot meet him: that's not so.
O, she is lame—love's heralds should be thoughts,
Which ten times faster glide than the sun's beams—' "

"*Assez!*" Grand-mère cried. "Enough! 'Cadie could read the lines better than that. What disturbs you, Lauré?"

"You—you're going too fast for me," Lauré confessed. "I'm frightened. What if I really have no talent? What if he discovers it now? And this play—I've never cared for it much."

Grand-mère sat down, nodding at her patiently. "Are you afraid, then, of facing the truth about yourself? Have you so little confidence in your own ability?"

Lauré was silent, and after a moment Grand-mère reached out to touch her hand lightly. "Don't distress yourself. There will be time. It is three days before your father will come. In that period you can rehearse the scene, acquaint yourself with Juliet."

"But this is the scene with the nurse," Lauré said, "and who is there to play the nurse?"

"Who but I?" Grand-mère demanded, waving the gold knob of her cane in Lauré's direction. "If I cannot play the nurse better than the Juliet you have just given me, then I am not the mother of Jules Beaudine!"

Arcadie had been listening to all this in openmouthed astonishment. Now she began to laugh softly. "Oh, it's a marvelous idea, Lauré. Grand-mère will be wonderful as the nurse. In New Orleans we are always giving plays among ourselves, and now and then Grand-mère still takes part and shows the rest of us up as very feeble players indeed. It will put you on your mettle to play Juliet to Grand-mère's nurse."

Lauré nodded. "I can see that. But what if my father listens and says I have no talent? What if he refuses on the strength of this one scene—?"

"Is it not better to know?" Grand-mère asked kindly. "Don't worry yourself—take the book with you and study the part. Later we will try it again, you and I. We can help each other, so that your famous father will not be ashamed of us."

Grand-mère waved her away, and Lauré went downstairs and out of the house with the book in her hands. She wandered toward the old *garçonnière* and sat down on the crumbling steps of the little building, the book unopened in her hands. There was more to this plot than met the eye, and she suspected that she knew what it was. Her grandmother had no great opinion of her talent as an actress. Probably she felt that no amount of study and rehearsal would bring Jules's daughter up to a standard that would demand respect and consent from a successful actor. Clearly this was a plan by which Lauré would herself bring about her father's refusal, and would deserve it. Then, as Grand-mère thought, there would be no more "nonsense" about going on the stage, and both she and Jules Beaudine would be pleased.

So that was it!

Lauré could feel the stiffening of her spine, the tightening of her will. Grand-mère did not suspect what she could do when she tried. What was to keep her from rising to the challenge and silencing them both, winning her father's consent in spite of himself? She knew he would be fair. He would not discount her ability if she really proved it to him. And once she won his consent, she need no longer worry about living with Aunt Judith, or about being left behind in New Orleans when her father went north.

She opened the book eagerly now, but before she began to read she thought about Juliet. Always before she had been impatient with Shakespeare's "star-cross'd" lovers. But now perhaps she could understand them a little better, because she herself knew something of love. It might not be so very difficult, after all, to lose herself in the part of Juliet and bring it to life.

This time she began at the beginning to read the play clear through, and now it had a magic for her she had never felt before. A blue jay scolded in a nearby tree, hoofbeats and the whinny of a horse sounded on a nearby road. But she did not raise her head until she heard a step upon the earth behind her and a shadow fell across her page. She looked up into the face of Cole Drummond.

"I thought you didn't care for Juliet," he said.

She stared at him in bewilderment, as though he might have dropped from a tree overhead, and he laughed at her expression.

"No," he said, "I'm not a phantom. And neither did I just happen to be passing by. My mother wrote that you were here at Les Ombres, and I drove over today in a buggy to see if I might take you for a drive."

It was so wonderful to see him that for a moment it was difficult to mask her delight. "I'll go ask Grandmother if I may," she began, but he caught her hand as she rose.

"Wait—tell me first why you are reading *Romeo and Juliet*."

She told him then—about her grandmother's plot, and of her father's coming visit. He listened attentively, his lips smiling, though somehow his eyes were grave.

"You'll show them up, of course," he said with assurance. "Don't let your father and Madame Beaudine shake your confidence and give you stage fright. If I may be invited, I'll come over to see your triumph."

Just the fact that he was ready to believe in her renewed her courage. "I *will* do it," she said. "I know I can, if I try."

As they started back together, Cole looked up at the old house admiringly. "They knew how to build in those days. Mother wrote me that your grandmother has finally sold it."

Lauré nodded. "What a shame that the old ways have to go."

"But necessary," Cole said. "We have to make way for the new."

Grand-mère heard their voices and came out upon the gallery behind the pillars.

"*Bonjour,* Madame Beaudine," Cole said. "I've come to take you and Lauré for a drive if you will do me the honor."

Grand-mère stared down at him for a moment. "As I recall, young man, you have completely lost the respect I once had for you. Why should I consent to go driving with you?"

Cole smiled at her. "Because I still value your respect, Madame, and I hope you'll give me a chance to redeem it."

Grand-mère's eyes were twinkling, and Lauré realized that both she and Cole were play-acting and that they understood each other very well.

"If you will wait a moment, I will make myself ready," she said. And nothing would do but that Lauré too must come in and put on her hat and gloves. It was an edict of Grand-mère's that no lady was ever seen abroad without hat and gloves.

Lauré had experienced a twinge of disappointment when Cole had invited her grandmother to come for the drive too. For a moment she had thought only of the pleasure of driving alone with him along a country road on this warm, bright day. But of course Grand-mère would never permit that. It would not be suitable, as she would say quickly, for a young lady of good family. So Lauré resigned herself to the company of three.

Cole's borrowed buggy was too small for him to invite Arcadie as well, but she didn't mind. Her eyes danced with pleasure for her cousin, and it was clear to Lauré that she was making much in her mind of Cole's visit.

Lauré herself did not know what to make of it. Probably it was no more than a friendly gesture on Cole's part. Perhaps his mother had suggested it. At any rate it was pleasant rolling along, with Grand-mère sitting erect between them, holding her parasol carefully over Lauré so the sun would not darken her complexion. A foolish precaution, because at every opportunity Lauré loved to bask in the sun, since she did not burn so easily as many blondes.

"Where are you taking us, young man?" Grand-mère asked as they trotted through the main street of a little town, still travelling west.

"I want to show you something," Cole said, but he explained no further.

Grand-mère spoke of her problems in getting Les Ombres into shape for its new owner, and Lauré was content to dream and pay little attention to her words.

The miles rolled by, the buggy raising a pleasant breeze in its passage as it followed the turnings of a little bayou. Then Lauré saw a small building of raw cypress wood ahead, as yet unpainted, but carrying, nevertheless, a look that was unmistakable the country over. The building was clearly to be a schoolhouse.

She glanced quickly at Cole, and he nodded in response. "Yes—this is the school where I'm to be teacher. Not very large, it's true—but it's a beginning."

Grand-mère murmured something about his poor dear *maman,* but Cole paid no attention. He secured the horse to a new hitching post and helped the ladies from the buggy. Then he led the way across bare earth, as yet unplanted with grass.

"People from nearby farms and towns have contributed the materials and the labor," Cole explained. "They're eager for a school for their children. I helped work on the building myself—so I know how well constructed it is."

He was proud to the point of boasting, Lauré thought, though the tiny structure looked pitiful to her eyes after the schools of New York City.

"In my day," said Grand-mère, unimpressed, "a gentleman never worked with his hands. It was not considered fitting."

Cole was taller than she and he looked down at her, laughing a little. "Do you think a lady is any less a lady these days for working with her hands?"

Grand-mère's fingers were covered by gloves, but for all that she rubbed glycerine and rose water into them every night, Lauré knew how red they were from scrubbing.

"Very well," said Grand-mère, changing the subject, "let us have a look at this place which is to make the poor dissatisfied by giving them an education they will have no use for."

What a strange mingling her grandmother was, Lauré thought, of the wise realist and the antique rule book of long-gone slave days.

"I don't believe," Cole told her frankly, "that the sentiment you've just spoken is your own, Madame Beaudine."

For once Grand-mère was taken aback. "It is what my husband always believed," she said defensively.

But now something had caught Cole's eye, and he moved away from them to stand beneath a half-opened window at the right of the door.

"That's strange," he said. "I'm sure every window was closed when I left here not two hours ago. I wonder—" He ran up the stairs and tried the door, but it was securely locked. Glancing back at his companions, he put a warning finger to his lips and then unlocked the door softly. "I think there's someone inside," he whispered. "Come in quietly."

The school was a one-room structure, and they stepped directly into the classroom itself. Neatly arranged rows of newly varnished desks and benches filled the center space. Following Cole through the door, Lauré saw that a little girl sat before one of the desks near the front of the room, her bare feet curled beneath her, her dark head bent over the desk. Her attention was upon her work with a stubby pencil and a brown scrap of butcher's paper.

"Hello, Lina," Cole said. "I was wondering who had scrambled in through a window."

The child must have been about Jessamyn's age, and she seemed no more dismayed than Cole's sister would have been. She looked up at him with eyes as blue as the summer sky, and as cloudless.

"It will be so long before school starts," she said. "I was pretending it started today."

Her lack of embarrassment grew from her trust in Cole Drummond. Plainly she gazed upon him as friend and hero.

She pushed the brown paper toward him shyly, and he picked it up to study what was written upon it. Looking over his shoulder, Lauré saw the childish scrawl, the letters awkwardly formed, but still clear enough to be read.

Over and over the child had written her name: "LINA EDWARDS, LINA EDWARDS, LINA EDWARDS."

"That is very good indeed," Cole told her. "I see you've remembered what I showed you the other day."

He introduced the child to Grand-mère and Lauré. She smiled at them uncertainly, suddenly self-conscious before such grand ladies.

"Lina," Cole said, "has come to Louisiana recently with her family, from Illinois. She was looking forward to going to school up there this year. Now she isn't so disappointed about moving to Louisiana. Are you, Lina?"

"This is a wonderful school," the child said. "It's brand new!" Her tone lent a spaciousness and dignity to the tiny building that made Lauré look about her with new eyes.

"You'd better run home now, Lina," Cole said gently. "And next time perhaps you'll wait till someone is here to let you in through the door. We don't want rain coming in a window to spoil our new desks."

The child agreed with a vigorous nod and started toward the door, but Grand-mère stopped her.

"One moment, my child! How many years have you?"

"I'm nearly eight," Lina said.

"And what will you do with this reading and writing you wish to learn?"

"Do with it?" Lina repeated, puzzled by the question. "Why—I will read and write. Mamma says that must be a wonderful thing. She says without it no one can amount to anything. When I am good enough, she says I shall teach her, so that she can read fine books for herself and write letters home to my grandmother."

"And when you grow up?" Grand-mère asked, her tone softening a little.

Lina spoke without hesitation. "Why, I will be a teacher, like Mr. Drummond. And I will go to small schools where teachers don't come, and I'll help other children to learn."

She bobbed a shy curtsy then, and ran barefooted out the door. There was silence when she had gone. Lauré moved about the little schoolroom with no more than a glance at her grandmother, fearful of what she might say. Madame Beaudine's hands were folded upon the gold knob of the cane, and her deep-set eyes looked far away as if at distant things.

"Lina is the Louisiana to come," Cole said. "Perhaps even the America that's to come with a new century."

Grand-mère touched the bit of brown paper Lina had left behind on the desk. "I am old and a little tired," she said. "It is fitting that the old should fight to preserve the past, though the young never believe that. We are the only ones left who know how important it is to remember a way of life that's dying. But perhaps it is equally fitting for the young like yourselves to do battle for the future—to build something out of the ashes of the past. Nevertheless, it is hard for us who love the old to recognize that the new really progresses. When I see places like Les Ombres dying, I am not sure this is progress."

"Not even when you remember how they were built?" Cole asked.

Grand-mère sighed. "I know. It was the labor of slaves

that made such grand living possible, and it is true that we progress from that. So too was the glory of Greece built, and it too had to pass." She turned to her granddaughter. "Come, Lauré. I am fatigued. Perhaps our young teacher will drive us home."

This time Grand-mère did not sit in the middle as before. She sat on the outer edge of the buggy seat and watched the passing scene sadly, perhaps remembering her girlhood once more.

Lauré sat next to Cole, sharply aware of his presence, of his hands upon the reins, of his strong, clear profile.

I love him, she thought, as she had done before. I love him because he is worth loving.

Today some of the excitement of what Cole wanted to accomplish had touched her. Now she could understand him far better.

17. A Cap for Juliet

COLE'S belief in her ability to impress her father began to fade in Lauré's mind in the days before Jules Beaudine's coming. Lauré studied the brief scene her grandmother had selected and went over it again and again, with Grand-mère robustly acting the nurse. And all the time her fear of what would happen increased. Somehow when she faced her grandmother and tried to speak the words, self-consciousness overcame her and she could not free herself of the inner shackles.

Nevertheless, she wandered through the peaceful woods of Les Ombres and spoke her lines to the squirrels and chipmunks impressively enough. And she did something else too. She learned by heart—and it was truly by her heart—the words of the balcony scene where Juliet first pledges her love with Romeo. She did not tell her grandmother that she was working on this scene; she wasn't even sure what she meant to do with it when the time came. But it was easy to learn these words, for now she knew how Juliet felt, the joy as well as the sorrow. Perhaps she could play the scene for Cole's approval, if for no other. He had promised to drive over for the performance the night Jules Beaudine was to arrive.

On the portentous day, her father came in the late afternoon when the columns of the house shone out of deep shadow and the waters of the bayou shimmered in fading light. Lauré and Arcadie were on the gallery when he arrived, and Lauré went eagerly to meet him. No one knew what Grand-mère meant to do—whether she would receive him privately in her room, or whether she would let him cool his heels awhile before she put in an appearance. She did neither.

When Lauré led her father through the wide main doorway, beneath the graceful fanlight, Grand-mère was just coming down the stairs. It was almost like a scene in a play, Lauré thought. As he went toward her, the old lady stood above him on the lower step and held out her hands.

"You have come home, my son," she said quietly.

Jules Beaudine, whose fame was nationwide, stood before her as if he were a boy again and unsure of himself. Grand-mère rested her cheek lightly against his for a moment. "Where have the years gone?" she murmured.

His arms went about her. "Yes!" he cried. "The years that have cheated us!"

"No, my son." Grand-mère shook her head. "The years *we* have cheated."

Lauré turned to Arcadie, for this was not, after all, a scene from a play, to be watched by others. The two cousins went outside beneath the trees and out of earshot.

"How marvelous that they have come together again!" Arcadie said in delight.

Lauré answered more soberly. "Yes, it's a good thing. But Grand-mère is right—the years are gone." Suddenly she turned to her cousin with a vehemence that startled Arcadie. "Oh, let's not waste our years like that, you and I!"

"But how does one know what is waste?" Arcadie asked wistfully. "How could it have been otherwise with those two?"

Yes, Lauré thought, that was the bewildering thing. How was one to know at a crucial moment what the wise course of action might be? How would she know? Once more there was a stirring of fear within her when she thought about tonight. It began to loom ahead of her as a dreaded ordeal. Dared she face the outcome? What if her father said she had nothing?

"Are you ready for the play tonight?" Arcadie asked, reading the doubt in her eyes.

Lauré would not put her dread into words. "Perhaps he won't let me perform for him," she said.

"He will do as Grand-mère commands—you know that," Arcadie assured her. "Besides—you will be wonderful. You will be so wonderful that he will beseech you to go into his theatrical company. And then I shall be desolate because you'll go far from Louisiana and never return."

Lauré slipped her hand through her cousin's arm. How

much of warmth and affection she had found in New Orleans! She would miss it when she went away.

All through the day her sense of dread continued and would not let her spirit escape its ominous grasp.

That night at dinner she could hardly eat, though the meal was a delectable one, cunningly planned to coax the appetite of Madame Beaudine's son.

The reunion was apparently a satisfactory one, and yet Jules Beaudine did not forget that he was an actor. He was overplaying a little, Lauré thought, and Grand-mère probably knew it. Was this what happened to all actors? Did they come to a time when they never knew when to stop acting, never knew who they really were?

Over rich Creole coffee Grand-mère announced her little surprise.

"We have planned something for your amusement, Jules," she told her son. "Something to turn the tables on you, in a sense. You are to play audience tonight and tell us truly what you think."

Jules Beaudine regarded her suspiciously for a moment, and then threw his daughter a look. She tried to meet his eyes without faltering—he must never guess how frightened she was. What little she had been able to eat of the excellent dinner lay heavy in her stomach, and surely her veins were running ice water. But she held at least to an outward semblance of courage.

Her father did not question or object. He merely waited, somewhat impassively, for whatever was to come. Grand-mère bore Lauré away upstairs and left Arcadie to entertain her uncle. Arcadie had her instructions and she would have him in the right place at the right time. So far, Cole had not arrived, and Lauré began to hope that he would not come. She could not bear to have him see the humiliation she feared lay ahead of her tonight.

Grand-mère seemed to anticipate nothing but success for her plan—whatever the word meant to her. She was as excited as a girl over her first play. She had laid out the things Lauré was to wear, garments that had been tried on at a dress rehearsal. When the time came she shooed Lauré off to her room to get dressed.

The old picture of her mother watched Lauré from a bureau as she discarded the many petticoats that were the style today and slipped the white silk gown over her head. There was a mantle of hyacinth blue to wear about her shoulders, and a gold cord for a girdle about her waist. In addition, there was something Grand-mère did not know Lauré had brought with her. From the pocket of her port-manteau she took the little Juliet cap of seed pearls that her mother had once worn, and set it upon her loosened hair.

Then she looked in the mirror with a sense of surprise. For all that the costume was makeshift, she looked as Juliet might have looked. Grand-mère came to the door and stared at her in silence. The old lady wore a white apron over her black dress, a white kerchief on her head by way of costume. The gold-headed cane would serve the nurse well as she hobbled about.

Lauré turned a little fearfully before her eyes. "Will I do, do you think?"

Grand-mère nodded soberly. "The cap adds a perfect touch. Where did you get it?"

"It belonged to my mother," Lauré told her, and nodded toward the photograph. "She wore it long ago when she played Juliet to my father's Romeo."

Grand-mère stiffened just a little. "You look the role, though Juliet should have dark hair. At least you are young and fair of face and as graceful as Juliet. Come—we'll go downstairs."

Jules Beaudine and Arcadie would be waiting in the great double parlor, where once gay parties had been held and Creole men had danced with beautiful Creole ladies. Now some of the furniture had been unshrouded, and a semblance of a theater set up. The end where the chairs were had been left dark, the other end lighted with candles and lamps.

Grand-mère led the way down the hall to the far end that would serve as the stage. "The curtain is up," she whispered. "Go out and give him your Juliet."

Lauré did not know whether or not Cole had come until she saw him sitting there beside Arcadie. But now she dared not think of Cole, or spare more than a glance for her father's cold face. Jules Beaudine would not like being trapped like this. But she must not think of that either. She must think only of Juliet. Now she was before them on the "stage," and of their own accord words were coming to her trembling lips.

" 'The clock struck nine when I did send the nurse . . .' "

As she spoke, the strange magic of the theater took place within her, and she was no longer a daughter afraid of angering her father and of humiliating herself. She knew Juliet so well. She knew all her tender thoughts and longings—they were her own. Here was a girl impatient for word of her love, impatient with an elderly nurse who doddered and took too long a time.

Grand-mère entered as the nurse and fleetingly, from the corner of her eye, Lauré saw her father smile. A brief smile it was, and quickly banished, but he looked less cold than he had before.

Juliet greeted her nurse:

" 'Now, good sweet nurse, —O Lord, why look'st thou
    sad?
Though the news be sad, yet tell them merrily;
If good, thou shamest the music of sweet news
By playing it to me with so sour a face.' "
Nurse: " 'I am aweary, give me leave awhile:
Fie, how my bones ache! what a jauce have I had!' "
Juliet: " 'I would thou hadst my bones, and I thy news.
Nay, come, I pray thee, speak; good, good nurse, speak.' "

The little scene was played through to the end, where the plan was made for the friar to marry Juliet to her Romeo. Then Grand-mère exited as she was supposed to do, expecting Lauré to come with her. Instead, Lauré stayed where she was, facing her small audience. She knew now exactly what she meant to do with the further scene she had learned.

She said gently, "Our scene is ended, but I would like to go back a little and give you something of another one."

For an instant she met Cole's eyes and saw encouragement in them. She did not dare to look at her father as she spoke the words of the balcony scene.

" '. . . O gentle Romeo,
If thou dost love, pronounce it faithfully:

Or if thou think'st I am too quickly won,
I'll frown and be perverse and say thee nay,
So thou wilt woo. . . .' "

She could hear her own voice going on in gentle entreaty
to the end of the speech. There was a moment's silence, and
then she was startled to hear her father's voice as he picked
up Romeo's words.

" 'Lady, by yonder blessed moon I swear
That tips with silver all these fruit-tree tops—' "

For an instant her confidence faltered. Jules Beaudine had
only to speak the words of a play to lend power to them. He
needed no costume, no stage to create the illusion of both.
Lauré caught her breath and answered quickly as Juliet.

" 'O, swear not by the moon, the inconstant moon,
That monthly changes in her circled orb,
Lest that thy love prove likewise variable.' "

It was a long scene, but she had learned it all, and they
played it through to Juliet's exit lines.

" 'Good night, good night! parting is such sweet sorrow,
That I shall say good night till it be morrow.' "

Lost in the role, Lauré moved blindly toward the door,
where Grand-mère stood astonished in the "wings." Behind
her she heard Romeo's soft words on her father's lips.
" 'Sleep dwell upon thine eyes, peace in thy breast! . . .' "

Then Arcadie and Cole were applauding soundly, and Jules Beaudine had left his place to stride after her, whirling her about before she reached the door. He held her by the shoulders so that she looked up into the strangeness in his face.

"So this is what you meant," he said, and there was excitement in his voice. "This is what you've been trying to tell me. Tonight you've shown me how much you are the daughter of Jules Beaudine!"

Lauré looked wonderingly into his face, but the spell of Juliet still lay upon her and she could not speak.

"I mean that you are coming with me. Someday I'll be able to bill us together as Jules Beaudine and daughter. You're untaught, of course. There is much to be remedied. But tonight, my dear, you gave us a true Juliet."

Lauré bent her head and could not look at him. Reaction had seized her and she was trembling. Her father's fingers touched the small cap upon her head and lingered there.

"You remind me of your mother tonight. How well I remember this little cap. But you are an actress, where she was not. Lauré, I won't oppose you any more."

She was too shaken to answer him or to thank him, too bewildered. She turned away and saw her grandmother in the doorway, a straight figure of outrage and astonishment—yet of defeat as well. Grand-mère's little plot had not worked. Instead she had been caught in her own trap.

Lauré went past her without speaking. She heard her grandmother protesting to her father, but she did not stay to listen. She wanted only one thing at the moment—to escape them all, even Cole, and get away by herself.

Out the front door she ran and across the gallery, down

the steps to the lawn. She did not stop until she had reached the *garçonnière* with its doorway hidden from the big house. There she dropped down upon the steps, wrapping her arms about herself to still her shivering.

18. The Answer

IN the house Grand-mère and her son were having a rousing good argument in the excitable Creole manner. Arcadie listened in alarm, but Cole had no interest in the outcome and he came seeking Lauré. He found her there on the steps of the *garçonnière* and sat down beside her.

"What's the matter, Juliet?" he asked. "You gave a beautiful, moving performance. You've won everything you wished for. I knew you were frightened and nervous at first, but you forgot that quickly. You had nothing to fear, Lauré. You have proved yourself."

She looked into his face, a little dazed. She had longed for approval, for applause, for her father's consent—yet now she had run away from these things and she did not know why.

"Your father is terribly pleased," Cole went on. "He'll take you into his company now. Come back to the house— he's waiting for you."

She wanted to say: "And what of you? Are you glad that I'll be going away? Or will you miss me a little, as Arcadie will miss me?" But she could not speak the words, so she let him pull her up from the steps and went back with him to the house.

There Grand-mère and Jules Beaudine stood upon the gallery. As Lauré approached the two, Grand-mère, who clearly had not yet accepted defeat, turned to her swiftly.

"So you think you have won!" she cried.

"You wanted me to fail, didn't you, Grandmother?" Lauré asked.

The old lady did not hesitate to admit the truth. "Yes, I wanted you to fail. I wanted to see you fail because only then could we know what you would do without your father's help."

"But she didn't fail," Jules Beaudine put in. "And there's no need for her to go on without my help. Tomorrow, Lauré, we'll return to the Drummonds' in New Orleans. You've stayed long enough in the Vieux Carré. And in a few days we'll go back to New York. I am rested now, and there's work to be done. I myself will take your training in hand. In the fall, perhaps you will be ready for a few small parts. Oh, not Juliet as yet, my dear. Not on a professional stage. You have too much to learn."

She could summon neither pleasure nor regret. It seemed suddenly that the earth was spinning too quickly for her, and she gave up the struggle to keep up with it. Grand-mère prevailed upon Cole to stay the night, and they all sat for a while in the parlor talking. With Grand-mère and her son present, there was never a moment of silence, and if the three young people had little to say, their elders did not notice.

When Lauré went upstairs to her room with the dormer window thrusting out of the roof, she did not undress at once, but knelt on the window seat in her Juliet costume, looking out into the bower of dark trees, trying to catch the shimmer of water on the bayou. All the striving had gone out of her, and she felt listless and without a goal.

Her grandmother found her there and came into the room in her loose peignoir, her gray hair in a braid down her back. She carried a candle which she set upon the dresser.

"I am troubled about you," Grand-mère said.

Lauré did not turn away from the window. "Because I am going on the stage? But now that you've accepted this in my father, why can't you accept it in me?"

"I accept my son—I do not accept his profession," Grand-mère said. "I am too old to change my feelings about the course he has taken. But that is not what troubles me. Do you remember the day when I asked you why you wanted to be an actress?"

Lauré nodded. "You told me I had given all the reasons but the right one that day."

"That is true. Tonight I want you to think about that question and its true answer."

Lauré roused herself a little from her spell of inertia. "But I know the answer. You believe I wouldn't work alone, without my father's help. But I have worked alone all my life. That's what you don't understand. When there was no hope at all, I worked and prepared myself as best I could. I learned parts and spoke them aloud whenever I could. I practiced before a mirror and—"

Her grandmother broke in with an imperious gesture. "And for what goal were you working?"

"Why, to be an actress, of course!"

"If you are sure of this, then I will oppose you no longer. Look, my child—I have brought you something."

A breeze caught the candle flame and bent it low for a moment. Then it flared up again to catch the shine of the chalcedony necklace she held in her hands.

"Come here to me," Grand-mère said, and Lauré crossed the room to stand before her.

The old lady reached out to clasp the necklace about Lauré's throat, and then stood back to admire it.

"It is yours, Lauré," she said. "I want you to have it."

Lauré touched the cameos in wonder. "But you said I should have it only if I pleased you. And I know I haven't pleased you."

"You please me more than you know, *chérie,*" her grandmother said. She saw the picture of Mary Beaudine on the bureau and picked it up to study the lovely young face. "It is my loss that I never met her. I know this now. But Mademoiselle Judith has raised you well. You must be grateful to her. *Bonne nuit,* my child."

Always before, Lauré had given her the name "Grandmother." The other had seemed too difficult to speak. But now it came naturally to her lips.

"Thank you, Grand-mère," she said.

Her grandmother took up the candlestick, and in the flickering light her eyes were warm and loving and wise. And there was a shine of something more than reflected light in them as she turned away.

"At least the years have brought me you," she murmured, and went softly away.

Lauré undressed and lay down upon her bed, thinking now of her grandmother's strange words, and of all that she did not understand. Tomorrow she would go away from Les Ombres. She would part with Arcadie and her grandmother—and with Cole. She knew her heart would break a little at this parting. Yet she would be going with her father into the life for which she had always longed and upon which she had set her hopes as far back as she could remember. So why was she not overjoyed? Why, why?

She fell asleep without finding the answer.

Early the next morning she was up before her grandmother was stirring, but she could stay in her room no longer. She wanted to be out in the cool, misty morning before the sun burned through to warm the day.

Cole was on the gallery, waiting for her. "Good," he said. "I hoped you'd be early. Come along with me."

Her heart moved in the first surge of joy she had felt since she had played Juliet last night. She had feared that she would never again have a moment alone with him.

He took her hand and led her along a misty path down to the edge of the bayou, where willow trees drooped green arms to the water. "I had to talk to you," he said. "I know that you have everything you want—now that all your dreams are coming true—and there's nothing I can add."

She faced him steadily, knowing the truth at last. "I have nothing I want," she said. "If I go with my father, I will give up everything that truly matters to me."

As she spoke, the answers were all there quite clearly and surely in her mind, and in her heart. All her life she had worked for one goal, but it was not the goal of being an actress. It was the goal of loving and being loved. That was what her early life with her mother and father had meant to her, and that was what she had sought so mistakenly to recover. Grand-mère had been wise enough to know. She had not given her grandmother the one right answer: that above all else she wanted to *act*. She had not given it because it was not true. She had wanted to be an actress because an actress was loved and applauded and approved, and because she lived that wonderful, happy life of back-stage. Those were the things the stage had meant to her. Louisiana had given her something far more true.

"I brought you here," Cole said, "to—" he hesitated, and then went on in a little rush: "—to tell you that I love you. From the first I've tried not to, because I knew you would only go away and I could never win you. But even though it means nothing to you, I don't want you to go without knowing."

Lauré knew her eyes were shining. "I'm not going anywhere," she said.

"But you are going to be an actress. You proved it last night. You *became* Juliet."

"No," she told him, "I'm not an actress. I became only myself. I know now why I was so frightened last night. I was afraid of winning, not of losing."

His arms came tight about her, and as he kissed her she knew that the years could never really roll back to her child-hood and the love she had known then. And she knew that she would not want them to.

"Do you think you'll be content as a schoolteacher's wife?" Cole asked, teasing a little.

"I'll be content as your wife," she told him, and knew her words were the truth.

Arcadie's voice, calling, reached them, and they went up to the house, hand in hand, as they had gone out from it. Grand-mère and Jules Beaudine were on the gallery, breathing the fresh morning air. Arcadie stood on the steps calling.

It was clear at once to those at the house that something had happened, though Grand-mère saw it first.

"I believe there is about to be a change in our plans," she said, and her eyes were bright as those of a young girl.

Lauré went straight to her father. "I'm sorry, but I can't go north with you to become an actress. I can't because I am going to stay here and be the wife of a schoolteacher."

For a long moment her father stared at her, and she did not know whether or not he was furious. Then his face broke into a smile, and he whooped in sudden laughter. There was far more relief in the sound than there was disappointment, and Lauré knew that he would not truly care. She would have been a responsibility to him of the kind he did not welcome and that he was willing enough to relinquish. Once this knowledge would have hurt her deeply, but now it did not matter. She did not need him greatly any more, and perhaps they would be better friends for that very fact.

Grand-mère broke in on her son's congratulations a little tartly. "So? A fine thing it is when the young no longer consult their elders concerning marriage!"

Lauré smiled at her. "But we are consulting you, Grand-mère. Will you please arrange this marriage for Cole and me?"

There was affection in her grandmother's eyes. "Perhaps," she said. "Though I do not promise, mind you. We shall see."

Behind them the old house brooded in a silence that was not unhappy. How many such romances it had known in the long years it had stood beside the bayou! And how fitting that there should be one more romance here in these shadows before the end was finally upon it!

207

Center Point Publishing
600 Brooks Road ● PO Box 1
Thorndike ME 04986-0001 USA

(207) 568-3717

US & Canada:
1 800 929-9108